jF

UCT

2006

0443077 84

CH

THE ROAD TO PARIS

Nikki Grimes

G. P. PUTNAM'S SONS

G. P. PUTNAM'S SONS

A division of Penguin Young Readers Group

Published by The Penguin Group

Penguin Group (USA) Inc., 375 Hudson Street, New York, NY 10014, U.S.A.

Penguin Group (Canada), 90 Eglinton Avenue East, Suite 700, Toronto, Ontario, Canada M4P 2Y3

(a division of Pearson Penguin Canada Inc.).

Penguin Books Ltd, 80 Strand, London WC2R 0RL, England.

Penguin Ireland, 25 St. Stephen's Green, Dublin 2, Ireland

(a division of Penguin Books Ltd.).

Penguin Group (Australia), 250 Camberwell Road, Camberwell, Victoria 3124, Australia

(a division of Pearson Australia Group Pty Ltd).

Penguin Books India Pvt Ltd, 11 Community Centre, Panchsheel Park, New Delhi—110 017, India.

Penguin Group (NZ), Cnr Airborne and Rosedale Roads, Albany, Auckland 1310,

New Zealand (a division of Pearson New Zealand Ltd).

Penguin Books (South Africa) (Pty) Ltd, 24 Sturdee Avenue, Rosebank, Johannesburg 2196, South Africa.

Penguin Books Ltd, Registered Offices: 80 Strand, London WC2R 0RL, England.

Design by Marikka Tamura. Text set in Cg Cloister.

Library of Congress Cataloging-in-Publication Data

Grimes, Nikki.   The road to Paris / Nikki Grimes.   p. cm.

Summary: Inconsolable at being separated from her older brother,

eight-year-old Paris is apprehensive about her new foster family but just as she learns

to trust them, she faces a life-changing decision.

[1. Foster home care—Fiction. 2. African Americans—Fiction. 3. Brothers and sisters—Fiction.]

I. Title.   PZ7.G88429Ro 2006   [Fic]—dc22   2005028920   ISBN 0-399-24537-5

1   3   5   7   9   10   8   6   4   2

First Impression

For Kendall Buchanan,
my foster brother,
and for the children of Royal Family Kids Camp.

PROLOGUE

Ask Paris if a phone call can be deadly. She'll tell you. She learned the truth of it last night.

The evening seemed perfect. To begin with, it was the tail end of spring, Paris' favorite season of the year. If you took a deep breath in the rainwashed air of Ossining, the spring green would pinch your nose with the tart smell of young leaves and the light scent of lilacs. You'd find a profusion of them right in the backyard of the brown-shingled box of a house where Paris lived. She'd clipped a few lilac blossoms for the table, and plumped them up prettily in a jelly jar. What did she care about fancy vases? It was the smell she was after. And, jelly jar or no, the fragrant patch of purple did a fine job of sprucing up the dinner table.

As she did every evening, Paris bowed her head while

Dad said grace. Keeping her eyes shut tight was another matter altogether. Jordan kept kicking her under the table. She shot him a few warning looks, for all the good they did. If he didn't stop kicking her soon, she'd have to order up a brand-new pair of shins. She wouldn't tell on him, though. She never did. After all, he was just being a garden-variety pest, like every other little brother on the planet, and that felt normal. In the world of Paris Richmond, normal was rare, and rich.

"Amen," said Dad in his rumbling bass. Mom piled spaghetti and meatballs on the first plate and sent it down the table.

"Oh! Paris, could you get the garlic bread out of the oven? I forgot it."

Paris hopped up from the table and grabbed the oven mitts. She'd forgotten the last time, and still had the burn marks to prove it.

She placed the foil bundle in a basket, peeled back the edges, and leaned down so the buttery steam could warm her face.

"Today!" snapped David, just to bug her. She whirled around and stuck her tongue out at him when Mom wasn't looking, then passed the basket to Dad, who was clear at the other end of the table from David.

So there!

Paris settled back into her chair, grabbed her fork, and put it to work climbing the mountain of spaghetti on her plate. That was when the telephone rang. Mom rose to answer it.

"Paris, it's for you."

Paris took a bite of bread, then went to the phone, licking garlic butter from her fingers.

"Hello?"

"Hi, sweetie," said a familiar voice. "It's me."

Paris held her breath. Time always stopped when her birth mother was on the other end of the line. *Why is she calling me? What does she want this time?*

Paris listened. Viola, her twice-divorced mother, had recently remarried. She wanted to give this family thing another go.

"Paris," she said, "I want you and your brother Malcolm to come home."

No! thought Paris, dropping the phone as if it were too hot to handle. *Not now!*

Paris rubbed the burn mark on her palm. In her mind, she knew the pain of it was nothing more than memory. So why did it feel real, again? And where had her perfect evening disappeared to?

Paris slid to the floor, leaning her full weight against the kitchen cabinet.

The phone cord swung out from the wall and sent the handset banging loudly against the doorjamb.

"Hello? Hello? Are you still there?" said the tinny voice on the phone.

"Paris, what's the matter?" asked Dad.

"Oh, Lord, what did that woman say to her? James, help her up," Mom said to Dad.

"Hey, Sis. Stop fooling around and get up," said Jordan.

"Yeah," said David.

Paris looked over at her foster family. They were all speaking at once. She could tell because she saw their mouths moving. But for some reason, her ears weren't working. Paris couldn't hear a thing.

4

Chapter 1

RUNNING AWAY

The trouble with running away is you know what you're leaving behind, but not what's waiting up ahead. Paris Richmond learned that a year ago when she and her brother Malcolm ran away from a foster home in Queens.

They slipped out of the brick two-story house one morning in late summer, hours before the heat would wring them dry. Malcolm moved free and easy in shorts and T-shirt, his head shaved cool and clean for summer. Paris, on the other hand, felt weighed down by the humidity. Her sundress kept her body comfortable enough, but her thick halo of blonde waves hung limp and heavy this time of year. She kept stopping to brush stray strands from her eyes, or off her damp forehead. Sometimes she'd rest her suitcase on the sidewalk so she could use both hands.

Paris trudged down the street after her brother, totally oblivious to the amazing swath of sky, a marble of sun-streaked clouds and marine blue patches. Her attention was on Malcolm's rapidly receding back.

"Hurry up!" said Malcolm. "Or we'll get caught. Is that what you want?"

Paris shook her head no. The last thing she wanted to do was get caught.

The foster home they were leaving was no place to be. The mother, Mrs. Boone, slapped Paris around every time her real daughter did something that called for punishment. You'd think she was playing some freak game of tag, and every single time, Paris was It. The woman never tried beating on Malcolm, though. But then, why chase down a ten-year-old who'd sink his teeth into you if he got half the chance when you've got a quiet, acquiescent eight-year-old to kick around?

Just last week, Mrs. Boone had grabbed Paris and dragged her off to the bedroom, a strap dangling from her free hand. Malcolm followed close behind.

"What are you doing?" he asked.

"Stay out of this, Malcolm," warned Mrs. Boone.

"You leave Paris alone!" he screamed. "She didn't do anything!" But the woman turned a deaf ear, locking the bedroom door behind her.

Malcolm banged his fists on the door.

"You better not hurt my sister!" he yelled.

Malcolm couldn't yell loudly enough to cover his sister's cries, but that never stopped him from trying.

After each beating, the daughter, Lisa, would swear she had no clue how her mama got the mistaken notion that Paris was the one who'd smashed a favorite vase, or stained the kitchen tablecloth, or whatever. *My name is Paris, not Stupid,* Paris would say to herself. And the last time Lisa made up a story, Paris called her a liar to her face. Lisa was shocked. Paris was rather surprised, herself. Malcolm was usually the one who did all the talking. Generally, Paris kept her thoughts to herself. She didn't want to give Mrs. Boone any excuse to lock her up in the closet again, like she'd done every day the first month Malcolm and Paris were there.

They'd told their mother, one of the few times she called, but Viola just thought they were making it up. No matter what Paris said, or didn't say, the beatings kept coming, and there didn't seem to be anything to do about them, except run away.

Early that morning, Malcolm snuck into Mrs. Boone's purse and grabbed enough cash for the train and bus. He and Paris tiptoed out of the house while the Boones were enjoying their Saturday morning sleep in. The streets were empty at that hour, except for a drunk huddled in a vestibule, and he didn't pay much attention to a couple of kids passing by.

Paris told her legs and feet to get a move on, and they did. Her suitcase kept bumping up against her leg, but she didn't care. She and Malcolm practically ran the last half of the block and set a dog off barking like crazy. Paris looked around to see if it was coming after her and almost missed a curb. Good thing Malcolm had waited for her at the corner. He caught her by the elbow before she toppled.

"Watch yourself," said Malcolm, in his grown-up voice. They hurried to the bus stop two blocks over and stood so long, their feet grew roots in the sidewalk. Finally, the bus came. Malcolm climbed up first to pay for their fare, then reached down for his sister's suitcase. On another day, she might have told him that she could do it herself, but not this day. Her arm was sore from lugging that battered old case. She handed it over.

Paris followed Malcolm to the middle of the bus. Soon as they were settled, she turned to her brother and asked, "Malcolm, are you sure you know where we're going?"

Chapter 2

TO GRANDMOTHER'S HOUSE WE GO

They were on their way to their grandmother's house in Washington Heights. Malcolm reminded her there was nowhere else for them to go.

Paris' white blue-eyed father abandoned her when she was four. Apparently, he couldn't handle being seen walking down the street with a child whose skin was so much darker than his own. He'd wince every time she called him Daddy in public. Malcolm's father had been even more of a stranger. He lasted less than a year. Malcolm had seen a picture of him, but that was the extent of his familiarity. As for their mother, she had no use for them. She was the reason they were in foster care to begin with.

Paris blamed it on drink. Her mother blamed it on loneliness. In a way, they were both right. Viola drank some when her most recent husband, Clark, was around, but she drank even more after he was gone.

Paris remembered clearly the night he left. They were sitting at the dinner table, plowing through mounds of mashed sweet potatoes, fried chicken wings, and green beans, too.

Clark polished off the first helping and belched without apology. He reached for more chicken, but Malcolm moved the platter, then smiled. If Viola hadn't been there, Clark would have smacked Malcolm, and they both knew it.

Whenever Clark had too much to drink, which was about every Friday after he got paid, he was in the habit of smacking Malcolm around, as long as Viola wasn't looking. Malcolm never told her, though. He figured it was something his mother didn't really want to hear. Paris didn't like it one bit.

This evening, though, with Viola in the room, Malcolm could do whatever he wanted, and Clark wouldn't dare touch him.

For a second time, Clark reached for the platter, and Malcolm pulled it away.

"Stop it, Malcolm!" snapped Viola.

Paris pressed her lips together to keep from laughing.

When Clark reached for the chicken a third time and Malcolm yanked the dish away, Paris burst out laughing.

Clark banged his fist on the table and shot up out of his chair.

"That's it!" he spat out. "I'm outta here!"

"Aw, baby," Viola cooed, "don't be like that." She snatched the platter from Malcolm, boring her eyes into his before turning back to Clark.

"Here, sugar," she said, holding the dish out to him. "Here's all the chicken you can eat. And I can always fry some more."

"Forget it," said Clark, heading for the door. Viola set the plate down, slipped past Clark, and blocked his path.

"Look, honey, I'm sorry about Malcolm. He was just playing. You know how kids are."

"Actually, I don't know. And guess what? I'm really not into raising somebody else's brats."

"Clark, look, if you want, I can send the kids to my mother's for a while so we can have some time alone. How would that be?" The more desperate Viola got, the softer her voice became. But Clark just pushed past her and disappeared into their bedroom. Viola ran in after him.

Paris and Malcolm stayed at the table, picking at their food quietly.

A few minutes later, Clark slammed out the door, suit-case in hand. Viola stayed locked in her bedroom for the rest of the night.

"Good riddance," said Malcolm.

"Yeah," said Paris. "Good riddance."

Clark being gone was nothing but good for Malcolm and Paris. As far as Paris was concerned, he was nobody her mom should be lonely over. And yet, Viola was.

That was when Viola started going to the local bars every night, where she drank to make herself feel better. Sometimes, that "feeling better" took days, and Paris and Malcolm would be left home alone. Malcolm did his best to take care of himself and his little sister.

One day, their grandmother dropped by during one of Viola's absences and discovered the truth. She called Child Welfare immediately, and Paris and Malcolm had been in foster care ever since. Grandma was the one family they had left.

One bus and two subway train rides after leaving Queens, Paris climbed the stairs of her grandmother's brownstone and rang the bell. A voice crackled from the intercom.

"Who is it?"

"Hi, Grandma," said Paris.

The intercom popped and sputtered.

"Paris?"

"Yes, Grandma. And Malcolm, too."

"Good Lord!" said Grandma. "What on God's earth has happened now?"

Chapter 3

SHORT TERM

Paris stepped inside her grandmother's apartment, the sweat of her brow quickly drying in the fan-cooled living room.

"All right," their grandmother said. "What are you two doing here?"

Paris pushed past the question, leaving Malcolm to explain. "Grandma, can I have a glass of water?" she asked. Her grandmother nodded and waved her off to the kitchen. Paris ambled through the apartment with more than water on her mind.

Her kitchen table's big enough for three people, thought Paris. *It's got two chairs now, but we could add one. The cabinet's full of dishes. I could help her wash them. I could even help cook, sometimes.*

Water in hand, she went to the bedroom next.

That's a nice-size desk. I bet Malcolm and I could take turns doing our homework on it. When Grandma isn't using it herself, that is. The bed's not so big, but the couch opens up. I'm pretty sure it's big enough for two. We could—

"Paris!" her grandmother called. "Get in here."

Paris hurried into the living room, slopping water as she went. She joined Malcolm on the sofa. *Yup, I was right,* thought Paris. *This is plenty big enough for the two of us to sleep on.*

"Malcolm told me what happened," said her grandmother. "But what he didn't say was why you didn't call your mother."

"Mother?" said Malcolm. "What mother?"

Paris gave Malcolm a look. "She hasn't called us for a while," said Paris. "And we don't know where she is, now."

"Good God," said her grandmother.

"Yeah, well. You know how she likes to move around," said Malcolm. "The longest the three of us ever stayed in one place was maybe six months."

Paris waited for her grandmother to say something, but at first, all she did was shake her head. Then she said, "Well, I guess you can stay here—for a few days. But that's it. I've already raised my kids. I'm too old to start that all over again."

"No sweat," said Malcolm, shrugging.

Paris studied her grandmother's face, though. *What's the matter with Malcolm and me? Did we do something wrong? Is that why no one wants us?* The words never left Paris' lips, yet somehow her grandmother seemed to hear them, and she looked away.

Malcolm and Paris swallowed up the first day running errands for their grandmother, watching television, and wondering what terrible place they'd end up in next.

The caseworker from the Administration for Children's Services had told the brother and sister they were lucky to be picked at all when they were placed with the Boones. There were few foster homes to go around, and fewer still willing to accept siblings. Paris did not feel especially lucky, but at least she and Malcolm had each other. That much she had learned to count on.

When night fell, Paris' grandmother made up the couch for Malcolm and said Paris could sleep with her. Boys and girls should sleep separately, she said. *That's silly,* thought Paris. *Malcolm's not a boy. He's my brother.* Still, she went along with it.

Paris was more tired than she knew. For two nights in a row, sleep rocked her like a baby, and carried her to a place of dreamless rest. When she woke up the morning

16

of the third day, it was to the sound of her brother screaming, "No!"

Paris rubbed her eyes, and climbed out of bed to find
her brother. Near the doorway, she found a tall, black
stranger pulling Malcolm by the arm, while her grandmother just stood there, watching.

Paris looked from Malcolm, to the stranger, to
her grandmother.

"What's going on?" asked Paris.

"Go back to bed," said her grandmother.

"Don't do this!" said Malcolm, trying to pull away
from the stranger.

"Who's that man, and where is he taking my brother?"
demanded Paris.

"Calm down," said her grandmother. "He's from
Children's Services. He knows what he's doing."

Paris looked at her grandmother as if she were crazy,
then darted for the door. Her grandmother caught her
mid-flight and held her firmly.

"You let my brother go!" Paris yelled.

Malcolm struggled to free himself, but the caseworker
held him fast, dragging him toward the elevator.

"Malcolm!" cried Paris. "Don't leave me!"

The elevator doors opened.

"Don't worry!" said Malcolm, tears streaming down his face. "I'll be back for you, Sis! I promise!"

The elevator doors closed while Paris screamed her brother's name one last time. Then he was gone.

Paris felt her grandmother's grip loosen, and then, suddenly weak-kneed, Paris collapsed in the doorway, sobbing.

Her grandmother sighed. "I'm sorry, child," she said. "But the caseworker said they had to separate you two. There was nothing I could do about it."

Her grandmother explained that Malcolm had been labeled "incorrigible," whatever that meant. From what Paris could make out, it had something to do with the money he'd stolen from the Boones. Paris tried to explain what had happened, that Malcolm was trying to protect her, that he'd stolen the money so they could run away, but all her grandmother said was, "Your brother's gone, and that's the end of it."

Paris wiped her tears away and balled up her fists. She found her grandmother in the kitchen, nursing a cup of coffee, and stared her down.

"I hate you," Paris told her. "You hear me? *I hate you.*"

Her grandmother said nothing. Paris stomped to her grandmother's room and threw herself across the bed. Anger was her partner for the rest of the day.

The next morning, Paris was on a platform at Penn Station, waiting for the train that would take her to her new foster home.

Paris' heart beat so loudly, the noise filled her ears. For the first time, Malcolm's hand was not at her elbow to steady her. His arm was not across her shoulders to calm her. His smile was not there to tell her everything would be all right.

The caseworker tried to hold her hand, but Paris snatched it back. She needed her hand to wipe away her tears. She'd never felt so alone in all her life.

Sometimes I wish I was like my name, thought Paris, *somewhere far away, out of reach. Somewhere safe down south or on the other side of the ocean.* Instead, she was neither Paris nor Richmond. She felt like a nobody caught in the dark spaces in between. A nobody on her way to nowhere.

The train rolled into the station, and she took one last look around before boarding, hoping to see her brother running to catch up.

Malcolm, Paris asked the wind, *where are you?*

Chapter 4

TRAIN RIDE

Paris ignored the caseworker seated next to her and pressed her brown face against the cool window of the train, staring wide-eyed at the Hudson River as the train raced across the rails, heading north.

Riverdale, Greystone, Hastings, Dobbs Ferry, Ardsley-on-Hudson, Tarrytown, Philipse Manor, Scarborough. Slowly, the cityscape gave way to the chiseled rock coast of the Hudson. The Hudson seemed one wide, wet boulevard separating the train and Paris from the other side of—what?

There was more open sky than Paris had ever seen from the streets of New York City. It was a view she would have loved to share with her brother.

Was Malcolm on a train going far away, too? Or was he still somewhere in the city? No one would tell her.

Paris fell back in her seat and wiped away a tear. Except for a sniffle or two, she rode to Ossining in silence. She wished the noise in her head would die down, though. Thoughts and questions were banging against each other like tin pans inside her skull.

What if they hate me? What if they beat me? Who will protect me? I could run away, but where would I go? I won't know anyone there. What if they lock me up like Mrs. Boone did? No, I won't think about that. Malcolm told me never to think about that again. Oh, Malcolm! I need you.

But there was no Malcolm.

Paris balled her fists, stuck them in her pockets, and closed her eyes. If she concentrated really hard, she could hear her brother's voice. Except now, that voice sounded a lot like her own.

Everythingwillbeallright. Everythingwillbeallright. Everything will be all right.

"Ossining! Next stop Ossining."

Chapter 5

MEETING THE LINCOLNS

Paris sat scrunched up against one door of the taxi while the caseworker chattered the length of the drive.

"You'll like the Lincolns," she said. "They're good people."

How would you know? thought Paris. *You never had to live with them.* But she said nothing. Instead, she stared out the window. The driver seemed in no particular hurry, cruising slowly through the small town. Even the people on the street seemed to move more slowly than folks did in the city. Paris couldn't decide whether that was a good thing or not.

They passed through a small square of shops and restaurants, then started down a steep hill. The sign read

"Spring Street," and near the beginning of it was a red-brick building with a cross on top. Star of Bethlehem Baptist Church. Paris liked the solid look of the place. It reminded her of churches she'd seen in Brooklyn.

"The Lincolns have two little boys of their own," the caseworker rattled on. "They also have a foster daughter who's a few years older than you."

The taxicab left Spring Street and wound its way to the final destination. Up they climbed along a hill that was nearly vertical, past two-story houses with sunporches and children's bikes strewn across the front walks.

The hill dead-ended right before a Con Edison power plant, but just below it stood a sweet old house. It was a two-story with brown shingles, and a whitewashed front porch wide enough for a bike, a tricycle, and the two-person rocker that faced the street. The dingy white fence that surrounded the house sagged in places, giving the house a relaxed and comfortable look, like an old slipper that was broken in and soft. But Paris knew better than to trust first impressions.

The caseworker paid the cabby. Paris followed her onto the porch and waited while she pressed the bell. Suddenly, the screen door swung open. A stout woman, near as pale as Paris' daddy, filled the doorway. She was black enough, though, and Paris would learn that hers was one of just three black families on the block, and the Lincolns were the only ones with kids.

"Well hello. You must be Paris," she said, very matter-of-factly. "Miss Liberty, yes?" she said to the caseworker. "We spoke on the phone. Please come in."

Paris entered the tiny hall, where she was quickly surrounded by several strangers.

"This is Mr. Lincoln, David, and Jordan, and that's Earletta," said Mrs. Lincoln in her clipped, all-business manner.

Before Paris could ask about Earletta's unusual name, the girl shrugged and said, "My mother wanted a boy. Guess that's why she didn't fight to keep me."

Mrs. Lincoln made no comment, but Paris noticed her give the girl's shoulder a gentle squeeze.

"Welcome, Paris," said Mr. Lincoln. "We're glad you're here." His voice was warm as hot chocolate, and just as sweet. Paris almost believed him. But when he reached out to give her a welcome hug, she jumped back. A look of understanding passed between Mr. and Mrs. Lincoln.

"All right, boys," said Mrs. Lincoln. "Give the girl some space to breathe. But first, why don't you show her to her room."

My room? How can I have a room?

"Okay. This way," said David, bouncing up the narrow staircase. Paris felt her suitcase slip from her fingers.

"I'll bring that up for you later," said Mr. Lincoln. Paris wasn't so sure about leaving her possessions with this stranger.

"That's okay," she said, grabbing her suitcase back. "I'll take it myself."

Mr. Lincoln nodded. "Suit yourself."

Reluctantly, Paris followed the boys into the belly of the house. At the top of the landing, she looked around, wondering which room was going to be hers. She'd never had a room all to herself. Why were they giving her her own room? "Girls and boys should sleep separately," her grandmother had said. But what about Earletta? Why wasn't she bunking with Earletta? Did Earletta have her own room, too? The house sure didn't look that big to Paris.

"Here it is," said David.

The older boy waved her over to the smallest room she had ever seen. It was hardly bigger than a closet.

The thought made Paris shiver.

At least there's a window, she thought. A twin bed hugged the wall. A rag rug lay in front of the bed, and a few feet away stood a desk and chair. There was a musty old wardrobe to hang clothing in, and, squeezed in next to it, an ancient dresser with peeling paint.

Now I get it, thought Paris. They were sticking her here in this little room to keep her out of sight, to hide her away so they could forget about her as soon as the caseworker left.

Paris looked dejected and the boys couldn't figure out why.

"You're lucky," said Jordan. "You get your own room!"

"Wish I had *my* own room," added David. "Then maybe I could get away from this squirt for more than a minute." Jordan punched his big brother in the arm, but Paris ignored them both. She swung her suitcase up on the bed and got busy unpacking. Bored, the boys headed back downstairs.

Paris sat on the bed, letting her eyes sweep every corner of the drafty room, wondering what the place would be like at night, wondering how bad it would be.

Fear was not something Paris needed to rehearse. "Frightened girl" was a role she already knew by heart. The question was, how often would she have to play the part here?

Chapter 6

FIRST NIGHT

Miss Liberty, the caseworker, said good-bye, assuring Paris that she was in good hands.

The rest of the evening was a blur. There was dinner, a litany of rules for Paris to memorize, then a brief tour of the house. Earletta gave her the tour, but only because Mrs. Lincoln told her to.

"This is the laundry room. That's the downstairs bathroom. Front porch. Backyard. Mom and Dad's room. The linen closet. The zoo, otherwise known as the boys' room. That's it! You've already seen the kitchen, dining room, and living room. And here's *your* room. But you already knew that. Don't get too comfortable, though."

"Huh?"

"You probably won't be here that long," said Earletta.

Paris turned around.

"What do you mean?" she asked. But Earletta was already halfway down the stairs.

Paris filed Earletta's comment away and crawled into bed, fully dressed except for shoes.

Gotta be ready in case I need to run. But where? Malcolm, I need you to tell me what to do, where to go.

Like a favorite blanket, or a teddy bear, Paris clung to thoughts of her brother. They were all the comfort she had.

The room was dark as a cave, even with the bedside lamp on. Paris strained her eyes in the direction of the dresser. Her suitcase stood right beside it. She'd left it nearby so she could repack in a hurry, if she needed to.

All in the house slept, except for Paris, who willed the hours to move faster toward dawn.

What will happen to me here? What if they lock me up in here? What if, this time, no one ever finds me?

Paris walked the tightrope of her fears for hours. Eventually, she missed a step and started falling, falling, falling to the ground. She flailed her arms, crying, screaming as she plummeted through the unending abyss. And when she finally hit the ground, it was morning, and she found herself in a tangle of blankets on the bedroom floor.

Chapter 7

BACKYARD BEAST

Paris slipped downstairs and out the back door to explore the grounds while everyone else was still asleep. Quiet escapes were getting to be her specialty.

Wow!

This was no postage-stamp backyard. It was a green and floral field to run in. The right was edged with hydrangea bushes, bursting with giant pink and blue blossoms. Towering above them were a smattering of trees rooted in the next yard over, and through the trees Paris could make out a silver snake, glistening in the morning sunlight, moving north to south. Of course, it wasn't a snake at all. It was the Hudson River slithering by.

The river the train followed to bring me here, thought Paris. *The river that could take me home.*

But where was home? Not with the Boones. Not with Grandma. Not even with Viola, because she never seemed to belong anywhere, in particular.

Home was such a funny word. For most kids, home was where your mom and dad lived, where you felt safe, where the bogeyman was merely make-believe. Home was where you knew every square inch of the place by heart, where you could wake up in the middle of the night and know exactly where you were without even opening your eyes. Paris didn't have a place like that. She didn't even have an address she'd lived at long enough to memorize, no single place that felt familiar as all that. Except maybe the city itself.

For Paris, home was more a person, and that person was Malcolm.

I could follow that river back to Malcolm. But how do I know Malcolm is even there anymore?

Paris kicked the ground and shook off the question. She had no answer and there was no way to find out the truth. At least, not yet. Paris turned her attention back to the yard.

Whitewashed arbors framed a small grapevine in the center of the yard. Here and there a few blue-black grape globes still held on tenaciously. Otherwise, Paris would have no idea what she was looking at. There were no grapevines on Lenox Avenue! The left side of the yard was enclosed by a picket fence, and in the back corner stood an old toolshed. There'd been one in the yard in Queens.

Wonder what's in there. Paris crossed the yard to find out. Her hand was on the doorknob when she heard a snarling sound behind her. Legs suddenly paralyzed, Paris slowly turned her head. There stood the scariest-looking dog she'd ever seen.

What was it Malcolm had taught her to do if she ever had to face a strange dog? "Never let the dog know that you're scared of him," Malcolm had told her. "Speak softly to him, and back away very, very carefully."

"Nice doggy," said Paris, inching away from the shed, trying to move past the long-toothed beast. "Nice doggy. Nice—ah!"

The dog knocked Paris to the ground and stood over her. Paris was too frightened to scream. She squeezed her eyes shut and waited for dog fangs to sink into her and rip her to pieces. *One. Two. Three.* Paris felt a mess of sloppy, wet licks on her cheek. "Oh, yuck!"

"That's Jet," said Jordan, slamming the screen door behind him. "We call him that 'cause he's fast. Did he scare ya?"

31

"Course not," said Paris, wondering if her heart rate would ever return to normal. "He's just a big ole fluffy dog."

Jordan came over and scratched the collie behind the ears. "Seems to like you," said Jordan.

Paris stood up and brushed herself off. "Nice doggy," she whispered, tentatively reaching out to pet him. *Maybe I'll be here long enough to get to know you, huh? What do you think about that?* Jet barked excitedly, as if in answer.

Paris stroked the collie's back, smiling for the first time in days.

Chapter 8

BREATHLESS

The second night, Paris experienced the Lincolns' nightly routine. When all the children were in bed, Mrs. Lincoln made the rounds, stopping in each room to say good night, switch off the lights, and close the door.

Paris was snuggled under the covers when Mrs. Lincoln suddenly filled the doorway of her tiny alcove.

"Good night, Paris," she said, hitting the wall switch and closing the door in one deft motion, leaving Paris to drown in a sea of darkness. The moon was no friend. The sliver of light that found its way through the window hardly made a dent in the darkness. Paris clung to her bedspread, her heart galloping inside her chest.

Just close your eyes, Paris told herself, like Malcolm had told her to do a thousand times. Paris pulled down the shades of her eyes and pretended all the darkness was behind her lids, that the room beyond them was really streaming with light. This trick worked for a while, and her heartbeat slowed a bit. Then she could swear she felt rough wool scrape her cheek. She flailed out, hitting nothing but air.

Ouch! Paris felt something sharp digging into the flesh behind her knees, but the sharpest things in the bed were her own fingernails.

Paris cringed. *What was that?* She heard a skeleton key turning in the lock of the bedroom door. Or did she? Real or imagined, that was the sound that undid her.

David was already snoring in the next room, but little Jordan was awake enough to hear Paris cry herself to sleep.

The next night was no better, though at least this time Paris knew what was coming. She dragged out her bedtime routine for as long as she could. She undressed, moving in slow motion. She slipped out of her skirt and hung it neatly in the wardrobe. She buttoned and rebuttoned her pajama top twice.

"You all better be in bed by the time I get there!" Mrs. Lincoln called upstairs. Paris bit her lip, wondering how on earth Mrs. Lincoln knew she was stalling. Reluctantly, Paris scrambled up onto the bed and waited.

When she heard the woman climbing the stairs, Paris felt her throat constrict. When Mrs. Lincoln reached the boys' room next door, Paris felt her skin crawl. By the time the woman approached her doorway, Paris could scarcely breathe. As the door closed, sealing off all light from the hallway, Paris gulped, longing for that scrap of light the way the hungry long for scraps of bread.

Once again, as much as she hated herself for it, Paris cried herself to sleep. This time, it was David who heard her. But fear finally drove Paris into a deep sleep where ugly memories stomped into her dreams.

"Let me out! Let me out!"

Paris pounds the bedroom door with her puny fists, but the door is locked.

"Hush up!" a voice hisses through the keyhole. "If you even think about crying to your caseworker about this, I'll come back and beat the black off ya!"

Paris and Malcolm huddle together in the middle of the closet, rocking each other back and forth, back and forth.

"Now I lay me down to sleep, I pray the Lord my soul to keep." Paris says this over and over and over again.

Tweedy jacket pockets scratch her tender cheek. She slaps away at the rough wool, whimpering in the cramped and stuffy space.

She and Malcolm take turns perching atop a rigid Samsonite cosmetic case. The cool brass fittings dig into the flesh behind her knees. A roach makes his way along her calves and up her thigh. She slaps her thigh to get it off her, but even after she knocks it to the floor, her skin still crawls. Her cheeks are streaked with tears, but no one is there to wipe them away except her brother, who has tears of his own.

Paris squeezes her legs together as hard as she can. She bounces up and down, she rocks, but it is no use. She has to go to the bathroom. Except there is no bathroom inside that closet, and she can't get out. Big girls don't wet their pants, but she can't help it. When she can't hold it in anymore, she cries anew and lets it go.

Paris roused herself from a deep sleep.

"Oh, no!"

Her bedsheets were soaking wet. She leaped to the floor, tearing off her soiled pajamas in a fit of anger. Shame burned through her straight through till dawn.

Chapter 9

SECRET

Paris made the bed that morning as usual, as if nothing had happened. When she went back to the room after breakfast, Mrs. Lincoln was there, piling the wet sheets on the floor. Paris wanted to bolt, but her feet refused to cooperate.

Any minute now, and Mrs. Lincoln would scream at her. The woman took a step toward her and Paris flinched, steeling herself for a blow.

"Next time," said Mrs. Lincoln, in her matter-of-fact voice, "you change the sheets yourself. There are clean linens in the hall cupboard. I'll change the bed this time. You put these in the washer. I'll be down in a minute."

Shaking, Paris did as she was told. She carried the sheets and pajamas to the laundry room and stuffed them in the washer, wondering what horrible punishment awaited her.

David and Jordan stared at Paris all through breakfast. She felt their eyes on her, but every time she looked up, they looked away.

Do they know about the bed? No. They didn't see me with the sheets. Their door was closed when I passed by. Wasn't it?

Paris did her best to avoid the boys for the rest of the day. That was easy enough where David was concerned. He went off to school right after breakfast. But Jordan was home all day, like Paris. He wouldn't be starting kindergarten until the next week. As for Paris, Mrs. Lincoln had let her stay home this first week to get used to her surroundings. That had worked out just fine for Paris, until now. She'd give anything to be out of Jordan's line of sight, at the moment.

When Jordan was inside watching television, Paris stepped out onto the front porch, and stayed there until he came out to join her. When he did, she ran to the backyard. When he showed up out back to feed his rabbit and to play with Jet, she went inside.

But her luck at avoiding the boys ran out when David came home from school. She bumped into him on the stairs.

"Why do you cry every night?" asked David, wasting no words.

"What? I don't know what you're talking about," said Paris, trying to push her way past the boy.

"Yes, you do."

"Excuse me. Can I please get by?"

"I hear you through the wall, every night," said David, refusing to budge. "What's that about? You scared of the dark or something?"

"Who says I'm afraid of the dark?" Paris burst out. "I never said I was afraid of the dark. Now, get out of my way. Please." The very idea of the dark made Paris shiver, giving her secret away.

"That's it!" said David, triumphant. "Little Miss City Girl's afraid of the dark! Man!"

Paris balled her fists and shouted at him.

"You would be, too, if somebody locked you up in a closet and left you in there all day!"

Oh, no! Why did I tell him that? I didn't mean to. Stupid. Stupid! Now he'll tell everyone!

That was the last thing Paris wanted. If anyone else knew, they might use the information against her, lock her up whenever they felt like punishing her.

"Gee. What kind of creep would do a thing like that?"

said David. "Hey, I'm sorry. I didn't know, okay? I'm sorry."

Paris dropped her voice to a whisper. "Please, don't tell anyone. Please. Promise me!"

David touched her on the shoulder lightly. "I won't," he said. "I promise." Then he let her squeeze past him and watched her disappear into her room.

Later that evening, after dinner, Paris was upset to see David whispering something to his mother.

He promised! I should've known better than to believe him.

Hours later, Paris went to bed. As she did each night, she shivered beneath the covers, dreading the moment Mrs. Lincoln would switch off the light and plunge her into darkness.

"Good night," said Mrs. Lincoln. Like a swimmer, Paris took a deep breath before diving into the deep. Mrs. Lincoln hit the switch. But something was different. When she turned off the bright overhead light, a smaller, dimmer spot of light appeared on the wall near the door.

A night-light!

"Sleep well," said Mrs. Lincoln, with a smile in her voice. She began to close the door, but left it slightly ajar for the first time. A wave of light from the hall added to the pool at Paris' doorway.

Paris sighed, relaxing her grip on the bedspread, and slipped into a peaceful sleep.

The next evening, when Paris and David were alone in the dining room setting the table, David said out of the blue, "I used to be afraid of the dark. And of the bogeyman, and of spiders—all sorts of things."

"Really?" said Paris.

"Really."

"What did you do?"

"I started keeping God in my pocket."

"Huh?"

"It's something my mom told me once. To keep God in my pocket."

"I don't understand. How can God fit inside your pocket?"

"No, that's not it. It just means to keep God close, you know, like he's right there, in your pocket, close enough to call on, or to talk to. That's what I do when I'm afraid."

"And that helps?"

"Yup. Sure does." And that was all he said on the subject. But it was enough. It was something she'd never forget.

Chapter 10

NEW SCHOOL

Paris tried out David's advice sooner than she expected. A few days after their conversation, she faced her first day at Claremont Elementary.

Standing before a classroom of strangers, Paris held her books tightly in the crook of her left arm, while her right hand was stuffed deep inside her skirt pocket.

"Class, say hello to Paris Richmond. She'll be joining us, starting today."

"Hi, Paris," came a smattering of voices.

"Paris! What kinda name is *that*?" cracked one boy. "And what's with the blonde hair?"

"That's enough, Brian," said the teacher. "Paris, take that empty seat in the third row."

Paris, whose legs suddenly felt heavy as concrete slabs,

finally made it into her seat after almost tripping, thanks to Brian, who stuck his foot out in the aisle when the teacher wasn't looking. Giggles erupted like bubbles all around Paris, but the girl sitting next to her leaned close and said, "Don't pay them any mind. They're all stupid. Jealous, probably, 'cause you're pretty, and unusual-looking, and you got a fabulous name."

Paris smiled in gratitude, wondering who this girl was.

"I'm Ashley," she said. "And you're Paris. We'll talk later."

Paris nodded, grinning at her new best friend.

At lunchtime, Ashley led Paris to the last table in the lunchroom, the one farthest from the door. That way, Ashley said, when the bell rang, they could take their time, and justify being the last ones back to class because they were the last ones out of the lunchroom.

"You sit here, and I'll go get our milks," said Ashley. She held out her hand, waiting.

Paris looked puzzled.

"You *did* bring milk money, right?"

Paris had never worried about milk money. Malcolm had always taken care of that.

Paris was trying to figure out what to do when she suddenly remembered the coins Mrs. Lincoln had pressed into her hand before leaving her in the school office that morning. Paris rummaged in her pocket and pulled out the coins.

"Here it is," she said.

"Okay. Be right back."

As the lunchroom filled, Ashley disappeared into the crowd, then quickly returned, balancing three cartons of milk on a tray.

"I'm extra thirsty," she explained as she plopped down on the bench. "So, where're you from?" she asked before biting into her spiced ham and cheese sandwich.

"The city," said Paris, slowly unwrapping her sandwich like the mystery it was.

"When'd your family move up here?"

"Well, they didn't, exactly." Paris folded back the waxed paper and studied her bologna sandwich, trying to think of a good explanation without getting into her whole family saga. "I mean, it's just me who moved here. Forget it. It doesn't matter how I got here. I'm here, is all."

"Oh, I get it. You live with your cousins or something, right?"

"Sort of."

"So, where do *they* live?"

"Riverview Road. At the top of the hill, up by Con Edison."

Ashley slapped her milk carton down on her tray, creating a pool of white in the corner. "Well, I'll be a monkey's backside!"

"Huh?"

"That's something my daddy always says," Ashley explained. "So, you live with the Lincolns."

"How did you know that?" asked Paris.

Ashley smiled.

"I live down the street, four houses over."

Paris laughed out loud. She could not believe her luck.

Chapter 11

NAT KING COLE

Paris didn't feel lucky when she had to do homework that afternoon, especially math. She groaned her way through it, though, one problem at a time. She was starting on the last subtraction when she was interrupted by Nat King Cole.

Music floated up from the living room. The song seemed familiar, and Paris strained to make out the words.

If ever I should leave you,
it wouldn't be in summer . . .

Paris smiled. It was one of her birth mother's favorite songs. Whenever it came on over the radio, Viola would drop what she was doing and dance to it.

One night during dinner, when Paris was about four or five years old, that song came on and Viola jumped up from the table and started dancing. She invited Paris to join her. "Come on, sugar," she said. "Dance with Mommy."

Paris had giggled, then let her mother drag her out onto the floor. The two of them danced from one end of the small kitchen to the other, while Malcolm laughed.

"Y'all look silly," he said. But Paris could tell from the brightness in his voice that Malcolm was enjoying the dance as much as she was.

The music was slow and easy, and Paris didn't have to worry about tripping over her feet, or getting dizzy enough to bump into things, so after a while, she closed her eyes and let her mother dance her around blind. It wasn't the least bit scary, though, because back then, her mother was somebody Paris could trust. Somebody she could hold on to. For a moment, Paris was lost in the memory of it—the memory of her mother, and the music, and the dance.

But that was a long time ago. Paris shook off the memory. The song was just a song, now. And the words of the chorus were a big fat lie. The singer promised to never

47

leave, but somehow Paris' mother had managed to find a way to leave her.

Paris went back to her math problem. She might not like numbers, but at least she could count on them to stay the same, no matter what.

Chapter 12

99 BOTTLES OF BEER

The first week at Claremont Elementary felt like a test. When Paris woke up on Saturday morning, she took a deep breath because she knew she had passed it. Or was it Claremont that had passed *her* test? Either way, Paris found herself thinking maybe this place would be all right. She couldn't help missing Malcolm, of course, but at least she felt a little less alone, now. She had a friend. Plus David and Jordan weren't half bad. David had looked out for her from the day he discovered why she was afraid of the dark. As for Jordan, it was kind of fun to have a little brother. She liked it when he needed her to help tie his shoes, or make sure his shirt was buttoned up right. She hadn't made up her mind about Earletta yet, but Mr. and Mrs. Lincoln seemed okay.

That afternoon, Mr. Lincoln made an announcement. "We're having a cookout. Last one of the season. Who's with me?"

"Me! Me!" said Jordan.

"Mmm, ribs," said Earletta, smacking her lips.

"Mmm, burgers!" said Jordan.

"If you're going to work the grill, James, I need to pick up a few things at the market. Paris, you and Earletta start working on the potato salad while I'm gone. Earletta knows what to do. Boys, you set the table."

David hunted in the kitchen cabinets for the checkered tablecloth while Jordan counted out the silverware.

Earletta put on a pot of potatoes to boil.

"What can I do?" asked Paris.

Earletta went to the refrigerator and pulled out a bunch of celery. "You can chop this up," she said. "And try not to cut off your fingers. I don't like blood in my potato salad."

That made David laugh. "Was I talking to you?" snapped Earletta. David stuck his tongue out at her, and continued setting the table.

Paris chopped the celery as evenly as she could, all the while wondering why Earletta didn't like her.

"Chop these, too," ordered Earletta, handing Paris a

pair of green peppers. Meanwhile, Earletta peeled a red onion over the sink under a spray of cold water.

"What did you mean that first night?" Paris asked.

"About what?"

"When you said I probably wouldn't be here that long."

"Nothing," said Earletta. "Forget it."

"Tell me," said Paris. "What did you mean?"

Earletta turned off the faucet, shook the onion, and laid it on a cutting board.

"You really want to know?"

"Uh-huh."

Earletta shrugged. "Fine. That room you're in? You're not the first foster kid to stay there. Five other foster kids have slept in that room."

Paris stopped chopping the green peppers.

"Five?"

"Five."

"Well, what happened to them?"

"Two got in trouble and went to juvie, two went back home to their mamas, and one turned eighteen and left the system."

"Oh," said Paris.

"So, I'm bettin' you're not going to be here for more

than a minute, either. I'm the only one who sticks, and I'll be here long after you're gone. So, like I said, don't get too comfortable."

Don't worry, thought Paris. *I'm never that comfortable anywhere.* She went back to chopping the peppers.

When the food was ready, Paris plopped down in the chair next to Mrs. Lincoln, licking her lips at the sight of that mountain of ribs, burgers, and toasted buns in the center of the table. She turned to smile at Mrs. Lincoln and she smiled back. That was when Paris saw a can of beer next to Mrs. Lincoln's plate. Mr. Lincoln had one, too.

Suddenly, Paris wasn't so hungry anymore.

After Mr. Lincoln said grace, everybody dug in. Except Paris. She nibbled and stirred the potato salad around her plate. A few small bites was all she managed to swallow.

"Paris, what's wrong?" asked Mrs. Lincoln.

"Nothing," whispered Paris. Her taste buds didn't seem to be working. They weren't able to distract her from the cans of beer on the table, or keep her from thoughts of her mother, whose drinking binges always began with a cool can of beer.

Paris felt a rumbling in her stomach that quickly moved up into her throat. She bolted from the table and, thankfully, made it to the bathroom in time. She hung her head over the toilet bowl and threw up until all that was left in her belly was air.

"Paris, are you all right?" Mrs. Lincoln asked through the door.

Paris rinsed her mouth out before answering. "I'm okay."

Mrs. Lincoln cracked open the door to see for herself. "I'll make you some tea and toast," she said. "That'll help settle your stomach."

Paris smiled weakly. "Thanks."

With her eyes on the floor, Paris returned to the kitchen and sat down. She sipped her tea and ate her toast in silence, then excused herself and went to her room. Mrs. Lincoln checked on her twice before leaving her alone for the night.

And a long night it was. Paris lay in bed for hours wondering how many beers were being guzzled, wondering when the yelling would start, wondering when Mr. and Mrs. Lincoln would storm out into the night in search of the nearest bar, wondering when she and all the other kids would be left home, alone. But the night was as quiet as any other. There were no sounds of fighting, or even arguing, to be heard anywhere in the house.

The next morning, Paris tiptoed downstairs before anyone else was up. She slipped open the refrigerator, found three remaining cans of beer. One by one, she poured the contents down the drain of the kitchen sink. Then she took the cans to the backyard and hid them behind the shed.

When she opened the screen door to come back into the house, she found Earletta standing there.

"If they had a drinking problem," said Earletta, "getting rid of their beer wouldn't help. I should know. I tried that with my last stepdad."

Paris pushed past Earletta without speaking.

"They like beer once in a while, is all. Not everybody who likes beer has a problem with it."

"But some do," said Paris, barely above a whisper.

Earletta sighed. "Yeah. Some do."

Later that evening, at dinner, Mr. Lincoln said, "I could have sworn there was some beer left." Earletta glanced at Paris, then looked away. Paris held her breath, waiting.

"Oh, well," he said. "Guess we drank more than I thought. It was good, though. Nothing like a frosty beer with ribs or burgers straight off the grill!"

"Got that right!" said Mrs. Lincoln. And that was the end of it. The subject was never mentioned again.

Paris sighed and felt the fist inside her unclench, one finger at a time.

Chapter 13

FUN AND GAMES

"Let's go, Paris," Mrs. Lincoln called from downstairs. "It's time! And remember, you have an appointment this afternoon with Dr. Stern. It's right after school, so don't dally. We don't want to keep the doctor waiting."

That's easy for you to say, thought Paris, retying her shoes for the fourth time that morning. *You don't have to talk to him.*

Dr. Stern was a psychologist, and Paris was in no hurry to go and see him. Who was it decided she needed to visit a psychologist, anyway? No one had asked her. And yet, an appointment had been made.

Paris sighed, and dragged herself downstairs.

"It's a routine visit," said Mrs. Lincoln, to soothe her. "Every foster child who's ever lived here has been to see the psychologist."

That didn't make Paris feel any better. She was forced to see a psychologist at the last foster home. Malcolm, too. That first time, he'd prepared her.

"Some of these guys are okay," he'd said. "They help you figure out your feelings and stuff. But then again, some of 'em just want to poke around in your brain, see if they can find anything to give a name to."

"What for?" she'd asked. But Malcolm couldn't help her there. He'd shrugged and told her not to worry. She hadn't. Even so, she hadn't much liked the stupid questions they asked. "Do you miss your mom?" and "How do you feel about her drinking?" and "How do you feel about your dad leaving you?" and "Do you blame your mom for putting you in a foster home?" Paris figured those were questions the shrink could answer himself. So why waste time asking *her*?

Mrs. Lincoln had set the appointment for 3:30 P.M. so that Paris wouldn't have to lose time from school. For Paris, that meant a day of watching the clock instead of the blackboard. Ashley asked more than once if Paris was feeling okay. "I'm fine," Paris said each time, flashing a phony grin.

When the final bell rang at the end of the day, Paris gathered her books and bolted from the classroom. Mrs.

Lincoln's car was already parked out front, and Paris climbed in without saying a word.

The drive to the doctor's office seemed too short; before Paris knew it, Mrs. Lincoln was getting her settled in the waiting room.

"I'll be back for you later," said Mrs. Lincoln, leaving her in the care of the doctor's assistant.

When her name was finally called, Paris said, "Here," as if she were in school. The doctor's assistant steered her in the direction of Dr. Stern's private office.

Stern was leafing through a folder, shaking his head, conferring with a colleague who was sitting on the corner of his desk.

"Jeez! Did you see this kid's file? Alcoholic mother, victim of child abuse, suffered abandonment—my God. There's no telling what dark thoughts are rolling around in that little head. I better make sure those foster parents know what they've gotten themselves—oh! Hello there."

Paris stood inside the door. Dr. Stern slipped the folder onto his desk and motioned his colleague out of the office.

"Come on in. Paris, isn't it? I'm ready for you now."

And I'm ready for you, too, thought Paris. *Since you think you know so much.*

"My name is Dr. Stern."

Paris said nothing.

"This is your first time here, right? So I want you to relax. Most of my patients manage to leave with all their fingers and toes." Dr. Stern smiled at his own joke. Paris did not.

"I see from your records that you've been to see a psychologist before."

Paris said nothing.

"So, how are things going for you at the Lincolns'?"

"Fine," said Paris.

"Are you getting along with the other children in the home?"

"Yes."

"Any problems you want to discuss while you're here?"

"Like what?" asked Paris.

"So, there are problems?"

"Like what?"

"Is anybody hurting you, in any way?"

Paris hesitated for a moment, studying the tweed carpet.

"There's Jordan," she said, at last.

"Yes? Jordan? What does Jordan do?" Dr. Stern leaned in close, pen poised over his pad, ready to note anything important.

"He kicks me under the table," said Paris in her most serious voice.

"I see," said the doctor, leaning back in his chair. "Well, that's normal for little boys," he said, sounding disappointed. "Anything else?"

Paris shook her head. She knew if she opened her mouth, she'd laugh out loud.

"So, basically, everything's fine at the home," said Dr. Stern. "Let's move on, then.

"Today, we're going to play a few games that will tell me something about you. Would that be all right?"

Paris nodded. She was looking forward to having a little fun.

The afternoon flew by in a whirl of tests disguised as games. Paris liked the inkblots best. As the young doctor flashed each card, Paris was to identify what she saw. When he showed her an inkblot that clearly resembled a butterfly, Paris said, "Elephant." When she saw a dragonfly, she said, "School bus." *Let him figure that one out,* thought Paris.

Next came a game of free association. That was even more fun. When the doctor said, "Black," Paris said, "Ice cream." When he said, "Mother," she said, "Sneaker." He scribbled notes furiously throughout, and Paris bit her lip to keep from laughing.

In the end, Stern placed an anxious call to Mrs. Lincoln, asking that she come in right away to take Paris home.

"Mrs. Lincoln," said Dr. Stern when she arrived, "please give me a call tomorrow so we can discuss a few things."

Mrs. Lincoln agreed, giving Paris' shoulder a squeeze.

That evening, when Mrs. Lincoln came to say good night to Paris, she lingered in the doorway.

"I bet I know why Dr. Stern wants to talk to me," said Mrs. Lincoln. "You were pulling that doctor's leg today, weren't you?"

Paris tensed up, wondering if she were in trouble. "Yes," she whispered.

Mrs. Lincoln shook her head, and laughed. "Exactly like Earletta," she said, more to herself than to Paris. "You'll do just fine, sugar," she said. "You'll do just fine."

Paris relaxed her shoulders, her heart beginning to thaw. "Thanks, Mom."

Paris' new mom switched off the light, the music of her laughter still hanging in the air.

Chapter 14

THANKSGIVING

Early on Thanksgiving morning, Paris went downstairs for breakfast, and was surprised to find everyone else up already, and busy as ants on a hill of sugar.

The sink held a mountain of yams. Earletta was chopping celery and onions. David was manning the toaster, putting in one slice of bread after another, then handing the toast to Jordan, who ripped them into smaller, bite-size pieces and piled them in a bowl for stuffing. Mrs. Lincoln sat at the table, snapping string beans, and Mr. Lincoln rubbed spices into the fat turkey.

"Happy Thanksgiving," Mrs. Lincoln said to Paris as she walked in.

"Can I help?" asked Paris, not really wanting to. This

many people in one space made her feel as if the walls were closing in.

"No. Not this time," said Mrs. Lincoln. "Why don't you check on Jet's food dish and make sure he has some fresh water."

Paris nodded and grabbed an apple from the fruit bowl on her way out.

The challenge for the day was not to get in anybody's way. Paris managed it by playing with and feeding Jet, taking care of David's pet rabbit, and reading a chapter book. She even raked up leaves in the yard without being asked.

At about noon, people started showing up at the door. Paris was introduced to each family member by Mr. Lincoln.

Grandma Lincoln came first, then came Mrs. Lincoln's sister Ida, and her two girls. Mr. Lincoln's baby brother Raymond, who was single, came next. Finally, Mrs. Lincoln's sister Jolene arrived with her nine-year-old son, Sheldon.

"We call her 'the mouth,' " Mr. Lincoln whispered to Paris.

The dining room table was packed. Mrs. Lincoln had used every extra leaf to make it long enough to seat everyone.

Packed or not, if anyone asked Paris, she would tell them that one person was missing from that table, and that person was Malcolm.

Mr. Lincoln said grace, then served up the turkey while Mrs. Lincoln started sending the rest of the dishes around the table. Sheldon, seated opposite Paris, stuck his tongue out at her as soon as he could catch her eye.

"Quit it, Sheldon!" snapped David. He leaned over to Paris and said, "Feel free to not like him. We don't like him much, either." He said it loud enough for Sheldon to hear. Paris was pretty sure Mrs. Lincoln heard it, too, yet for some reason, she let it pass without comment.

Paris concentrated on loading her plate up with candied yams, a few string beans for color, corn pudding, stuffing, cranberry sauce, and turkey. She took a swallow of eggnog before digging in.

"So," said Sheldon's mother, Jolene. "This is the new one, huh? My God, Sis, you collect sick kids like strays."

Paris choked on her eggnog.

Mrs. Lincoln banged the table with her fist.

"They are not sick, and they are not strays!" she said, between tight lips.

Earletta patted Paris on the back until she stopped coughing.

"Don't mind Aunt Jolene," whispered Earletta. "She can't help herself. She was raised by wolves. That's why she knows so much about stray dogs."

Paris managed to smile at that. She spent the rest of the afternoon avoiding Jolene and Sheldon, though. Those two were poisonous. It was hard for Paris to believe that they were part of the Lincoln clan at all.

After the main meal, the kids raced to the park at the foot of the hill and arranged a game of softball. Uncle Raymond joined them, and for once so did Earletta. David knocked at several neighbors' doors and picked up a few more kids along the way.

When they set up teams, Sheldon decided to sit out the game. He said softball was a stupid game, but David told her the real reason was that Sheldon couldn't play for spit, and he was the world's sorest loser.

Paris was happy to be included. She had an okay time, too, even though she never got a home run. She couldn't quite shake off Jolene's comment, and Sheldon didn't help. Everytime he caught her looking at him, he'd say, "What you lookin' at, Foster?" He wouldn't call her by her name, just Foster, short for *foster child*. Not once did he or his mother let her forget that she was an outsider, that she didn't belong, that this new home of hers was borrowed.

Back at the house, Paris stuffed her feelings with fresh-baked pumpkin pie and ice cream, having seconds, and even thirds.

Now, she was too stuffed to sleep. She lay awake for a long time, hearing Sheldon's taunting voice in her head, calling her Foster. It was enough to give her a bellyache. And it did.

Chapter 15

ADDRESS UNKNOWN

Dear Malcolm,

I miss you everyday.

I'm living in a place called Ossining. Ever hear of it? It took a long train ride to get here. Its got a famus prison. Sing Sing. What a funny name for a place where they lock you up. I bet nobody who lives there sings. I wouldn't.

The house I'm in is nothing like a prison. They don't beat me here, Malcolm. Not so far. Or lock me up in closets. You know what? The people here are preety nice, except for one aunt and one cousin. But they're not worth talking about.

Mrs. Lincoln, the mom, is a big lady, but not jolly at all. She's crusty as burnt toast on the outside, but inside, she's all soft and sweet as pudding. Mr. Lincoln is quiet, mostly. I only see him at breakfast and at night after work. But you always know when he's in the house, cause the whole house calms down. Even Jet.

Jet's the dog. Well, he's practically a pony, he's so big! He's not scarey or anything. He's like a big, fluffy kid who wants to play all the time. You would like him alot.

There are two boys, so I've still got brothers to pester me. (smile). David is the oldest, and Jordan is the baby. David is helping me so I don't have to be afraid of the dark all the time. Jordan hangs onto me sometimes like I'm really his big sister. He's cute. Did I used to hang onto you like that? I feel like I'm starting to forget. I'm sorry, Malcolm.

There's a girl here called Earletta. But I don't see her much. She's real old like in high school and doesn't want to hang around with a kid my age. Which I don't mind. I like to stay to myself, anyway. I get to do that a lot cause—surprise!—I have my own room. Would you believe it? Its a teeny room, tho. I don't want you thinking I'm in some palace. Still, I wish you were here to share it.

Where are you? I'm writing this stupid letter and I don't even know where to send it. I had to talk to you, tho, even if its only on paper.

I better go. Its my turn to set the table. (I have chores now, like you used to have at home before Mom—never mind. I don't think about her anymore, or grandma who I'm still mad at.)

Oh! I almost forgot. I have a new friend. Her name is Ashley. She lives down the street.

Bye for now.

Paris.

Chapter 16

MARCHING TO ZION

Paris decided it was time to try out the family church. Mrs. Lincoln didn't make Paris go when she first got to Ossining. Paris was left to decide when she was ready. "God won't force you to visit his house," said Mrs. Lincoln, "and I won't, either." That was fine with Paris because there was already so much new to get used to.

One Sunday morning, Paris woke up feeling ready to go.

Star of Bethlehem Baptist Church was lovely inside, with its beautiful stained-glass windows and rich wood accents, but it felt like somebody had forgotten to turn the heat on. The wooden pews were cold against Paris' thighs. She couldn't understand for the life of her why she couldn't wear pants to church. She didn't see David and Jordan freezing their legs off. Who made the rule that girls had to wear dresses to church, anyway?

Paris tried to express this point over breakfast, but Mrs. Lincoln stopped her with one of those deadpan stares, and said, "Paris Richmond, who told you life was fair?" And that was the end of the discussion.

Paris sat swinging her legs, pouting—until she heard the first chords of the organ. The sound sent an electric spark up one pew and down the next, and Paris forgot all about being cold. The melody flowed into her body like liquid sunshine, warming her as it traveled from the tips of her ears to the tips of her toes. Paris never knew that such a sound existed.

"Are you okay?" asked Mr. Lincoln. Paris, her lips slightly parted, nodded and went on listening. She didn't know how to explain it, but as the music played, she felt herself waking up inside.

"All rise," said a voice up front. The organist switched music and began to play "Marching to Zion." The choir marched in from the back of the sanctuary, stepping in time to the music. When the choir loft was filled, the organist changed the melody once more. "Nothing but the Blood," then "What a Friend We Have in Jesus," and "Give Me Jesus on the Line." He played one song after another, and the choir rode the sturdy waves of the organ music, their voices piercing the rafters and raising the temperature of everyone in the room.

The music was all Paris heard that first morning at Star of Bethlehem. The prayers and sermon in between were merely interruptions. It was the music that spoke to Paris, the music she couldn't wait to hear next. Mr. Lincoln couldn't help but notice.

At the end of the service, he leaned down to Paris. "You know," he said, very casually, "we have a youth choir here. Think you might like to join it?"

Paris all but leapt off the pew seat in response.

"Could I?"

Mr. Lincoln smiled. "Of course. Brother Wilson?" he called to the choir director. "I need to see you for a moment. I've got a new choir member here for you."

Paris couldn't stop grinning. The idea of singing in the choir put a sparkle in her eyes that lasted for days.

Chapter 17

JINGLE BELLS

Christmas, Christmas, Christmas. That was all anybody talked about at school. Paris couldn't even get away from it during lunch. Take this afternoon, for instance.

When Paris and her classmates filed into the cafeteria, they found the walls plastered with paper snowflakes, drawings of Christmas trees, and pictures of Santa with a beard made from cotton balls.

"I can't wait till Christmas break," said a boy named Warren.

"Me neither," said Ashley.

"You guys are lucky," said Warren's buddy, Brad. "You get to stay home for Christmas. My dad is dragging us to California to visit our cousins so we can have a Christmas barbecue on the beach! How lame is that?"

"Sounds like fun!" said Ashley.

"You gotta be kiddin'!" said Brad. "Who ever heard of Christmas without snow?"

"People in Hawaii," said Lee Young. "And parts of Africa."

"All I'm sayin' is, Christmas is not the same without snow," Brad continued to argue.

"Forget the snow," said Brian. "I can't wait to see what presents I get."

"I love putting up the tree," said Ashley. "And driving around town to see all the lights on people's houses."

"And the Nativity scenes," said a girl named Lori.

"Yeah!" said Ashley.

"Last year," said Warren, "my church had a living Nativity and my baby sister was Jesus."

"Stop lying!" said Brian. "How they gonna use a girl baby to play Jesus?"

"At that age, it don't make much difference," said Warren. "Wrap them up in a blanket, and all babies look the same."

Their lunch trays full, the group split off to find seats with their friends. Paris and Ashley found two free spaces and sat together.

"What's the matter?" Ashley asked Paris.

"Nothing," said Paris, pasting a smile on her face.

"You're awfully quiet," said Ashley. "Is something wrong?"

"No. I'm fine," said Paris.

Except I miss Malcolm more than ever.

For Paris, the best thing about Christmas was being with her brother. And this Christmas, she didn't even know where he was.

Paris ate her lunch in silence, nodding occasionally as Ashley chattered on about the holiday.

Christmas might as well be just another day, as far as Paris was concerned. Viola certainly didn't seem to notice it. Either that or she didn't care. Every afternoon, Paris ran to check the mail hoping to find a package, or at least a card from her mother. Every evening, Paris waited for the phone to ring, hoping to find her mother on the other end. But every afternoon and evening ended in disappointment.

It doesn't matter, Paris would tell herself. Then she'd put Viola out of her mind for a while, because thinking about her hurt too much.

All the Lincolns were extra nice to Paris, making sure to include her in their family traditions. Like dragging her to the Christmas tree farm.

Paris didn't want to go, but she didn't want to make

Mrs. Lincoln feel bad. Once she got there, out in the crisp pine-washed air, it wasn't half bad. And the trees were worth seeing, taller and fatter than any Paris had ever seen at storefronts in New York City.

"Aren't they great?" said David, grinning.

"They're okay," said Paris.

"Okay? Are you blind?"

David shook his head and ran down the rows of evergreens, Jordan fast on his heels. Paris could hear Jordan's squeals of excitement as he and David ran from tree to tree, trying to decide which was the best. It seemed to take forever before they chose one.

Back home, everyone pitched in, decorating the tree while Paris watched from the sidelines. The one thing she seemed to enjoy was the Christmas music playing on the stereo. As long as that was on, she sat in the living room with the rest of the family, humming along with the record.

On Christmas morning, Paris found a few presents under the tree with her name on them, marked "From Santa." Santa was as boring as her grandmother: he'd given her socks, pink earmuffs (Paris hated pink), and mittens. Paris said thank you to the Lincolns, wishing she had more than a card for them.

"The card is beautiful," said Mrs. Lincoln. "But you know what else I want for Christmas that you can give me? A song."

Paris didn't think that was much of a present, but she sang anyway. "Jingle Bells" was the first song she could think of, so that was what she sang. There wasn't much joy in her voice, though.

The one highlight that first Christmas was trading gifts with Ashley, who'd come over that afternoon for a little while.

Paris was in her room, finishing a letter to Malcolm, when the doorbell rang.

"Paris!" called Mrs. Lincoln. "Ashley's here."

By the time Paris put down her pen and paper, a beaming Ashley lit up her doorway, a shopping bag dangling from one hand.

"Merry Christmas!" said Ashley.

"Merry Christmas."

"I'd have come over sooner, but my mom made me wait. 'Folks like to start their Christmas mornings off slow and easy,' she said. I swear, I don't know *where* she gets these ideas."

Paris grinned. Ashley could always put a smile on her face.

"Anyway," said Ashley, plopping down on Paris' bed, "here I am."

Ashley pulled a long, narrow box from her shopping bag. The box was wrapped in silver foil.

"This is for you," she said, holding the box out toward Paris, looking as if she were about to burst. "Go on! Open it!"

"Wait," Paris said. She went to her desk and pulled a small, flat package from the drawer.

"You first," she said, a little anxious. Since Paris didn't have any money, she'd made a gift for her friend. "I hope you like it," she said.

Ashley tore the wrapping paper and ripped off the lid of the box. Paris held her breath.

"Oh, wow!" said Ashley, staring down at a square of denim.

"It's a book cover," said Paris, explaining in a tumble of words. "I made it from an old pair of jeans, Earletta helped me stitch the edges, I sewed the buttons on the front myself."

"I love it!" said Ashley. She turned the cover over in her hands, feeling the smooth edges and tracing the metal buttons with a fingertip.

"The buttons are the best part," she said. Paris beamed.

"Okay. Now it's your turn," said Ashley.

Paris picked up the narrow package, held it to her ear, and shook it, hoping for a clue to its contents.

"Open it! Open it!" said Ashley, bouncing up and down on the bed.

Slowly and delicately, Paris unwrapped the package, folding back each corner of the wrapping paper with great care.

"You're killing me!" said Ashley, groaning.

Paris had never gotten that many presents at Christmas, so she wanted to make the most of every one. When she finally folded back the tissue paper, her heart skipped a beat. Nestled inside the box was a small wooden flute.

"I know how much you like music," said Ashley. "So, hurry up and figure out how this thing works so you can play me something."

Paris was speechless.

"Well, I gotta go now," said Ashley in a soft voice. "I'm glad you like your present. I'll see you later."

Paris clutched the flute in her hand, gave her friend a long, hard hug, then walked her to the door.

Chapter 18

FORT FRIENDLY

The next day at church, Paris belted out the Christmas hymns with a secret joy. Singing in the choir was sweeter than hot chocolate with swirls of whipped cream. All too soon, the service was over and it was time to leave.

The drive home was treacherous. While Paris was in church, it was as if God had sunk his shovel into a mountain of snow and scattered it over the whole earth.

Snow continued to fall all day and through the night. When Paris woke up the next morning, the little house on the hill was an island surrounded by a silent sea of white.

Wow, thought Paris.

She had never seen so much snow.

Her bedroom door flew open, and David stuck his head inside.

"Snow day!" he said, grinning. "I'll bet you anything!" Then he took off down the stairs.

Paris threw on her robe, jumped into her slippers, and went to investigate. She found the family sitting around the breakfast table, craning toward the kitchen radio, which was up full volume. Mr. Lincoln would have turned it down, had he been there. But he'd headed out the night before for a late shift at Con Edison. A short walk up the steep hill got him there, so his car was still in the driveway. The overnight snowfall had completely covered his tracks.

The radio crackled, catching Paris' attention. *"Ignatious Elementary: closed. McKinley Elementary: closed. Claremont Elementary: closed."*

"Wahoo!" sang David and Jordan in chorus. Mrs. Lincoln groaned. So did Earletta. Her school was also closed, and the thought of spending a day at home with her pesky little brothers wasn't her idea of fun.

"All right, boys," said Mrs. Lincoln. "Get your clothes on. You, too, Paris. I need you to clear the snow from the doorway, and clear a path down the front steps. Then you can play."

"How come Earletta isn't helping?" asked Paris.

"I am *not* climbing through anybody's window," said Earletta.

Paris was puzzled. "Window?"

...

A few minutes later, Paris opened the front door. That was as far as she got. The screen door was wedged shut by two and a half feet of snow. The only way out of the house was through a window.

"Climb on out, then make your way to the backyard," said Mrs. Lincoln. "There are shovels in the shed. David knows where we keep them."

The boys climbed out first to show her there was nothing to it. "Stuff your pant legs all the way inside your boots," David instructed. "That'll make it easier for you to walk."

Paris did as she was told, then hoisted herself through the living room window. She sank into a mound of cold, then stood a long while transfixed by the alien landscape.

The entire street was smothered in snow, right up to the doorways of each house. Gone were streets and sidewalks. Driveways were invisible. Telephone wires hung heavy, looking every bit like clotheslines draped with wet, white laundry. Mailboxes and telephone poles were skinny islands in a sea of powder. The house across the street looked like a gingerbread house with powdered sugar on the rooftop. She'd never seen anything like it in the city.

Does our house look like that, too? Paris wondered. She

closed her eyes, smiling at the hushed sound of it all, rocking in the waves of white silence.

"Hurry up," said David, bringing her back to the task at hand. "We have to get the shovels."

Paris thought it was a shame to disturb all that perfection, but she planted her boots into the snow, one step after another, creating a trail of fat footsteps even the man in the moon could see, all the way to the back of the house. David had the shed open by the time she got there. He handed out shovels and work instructions like a foreman. The littlest shovel went to Jordan.

"Jordan, you help Jet clear a path around his doghouse. He's already gotten started, so it shouldn't be too bad. Paris, you're with me. We gotta clear the porch."

Paris nodded, grabbing the shovel he held out to her. She followed David back to the front of the house, surprised when he came to a halt a foot short of the porch steps.

"What?"

David looked down at the snow, then off into the distance. "I got an idea," he said. "Help me."

David walked to about where the end of the sidewalk should be, to the right of the house, facing the downward slope. He sank his shovel as deep as it would go, then started shoveling. But instead of shoveling in a straight line, he worked in a semicircle.

Paris stood watching him. She had no idea what he was doing. "What about the stairs?" she asked.

"The stairs can wait. You gonna help me or not?"

Paris didn't want to get in trouble, but David sure looked like he was having fun. He began to shape the snowdrifts into a wall, pressing the snow together to pack it tightly.

Paris finally jumped in to give him a hand. She pressed handfuls of snow together like rough bricks, and stacked them atop one another until her part of the wall was finished. Then she and David stepped back to admire their work.

"This'll be the best snow fort ever!" said David. Now all they needed were a few more kids to play with, and their first snowball fight of the season was on!

"David Allen Lincoln," said his mother, arms akimbo behind the screen door, "if you don't clear the snow away from this door in the next five minutes, you won't be able to sit down until summer. That goes for you, too, Paris."

Paris and David looked at each other, biting their lips to keep from giggling. David gave Paris a wink.

"Yes, ma'am," said David.

"Yes, ma'am," echoed Paris.

Then the two of them got busy shoveling and salting down the front steps.

Threat or no, Paris liked having a new partner in crime. And if she did get a spanking, it would be for something she'd actually done, this time. And she wouldn't be the only one getting whipped, either. That was a difference she could live with.

Chapter 19

WHAT HEARTS

Paris checked off the items on her bedroom desk. Scissors, glue, gold stars, red and white construction paper, white paper doilies, red ribbon, crayons, Red Hots, and newspaper.

She got busy making valentines for her teacher and for Ashley, the one close friend she'd made so far.

One friend's better than none, she told herself.

Paris cut a big heart out of newspaper print, then a smaller one of red paper to put on top of it, then a smaller one out of a white doily to put on top of that.

Paris fingered the newspaper and smiled, knowing Ashley would laugh when she saw her valentine. Ashley must have told Paris the same joke a million times: *"What's black and white and red all over? A newspaper! Get it?"*

To make the valentine even more special, Paris counted out seven Red Hots to glue around the edges. Red Hots were Ashley's favorite candy.

"Paris," called Mrs. Lincoln, "dinner."

"In a minute!" said Paris. But one minute quickly became fifteen, because Paris was already lost in the sticky world of cut paper and Elmer's glue.

"Good morning, class," said Paris' teacher the next day.

"Good morning, Miss Broadnax," said the class.

"Who can tell me what today is?"

Brian rolled his eyes. He was always rolling his eyes. *One day,* thought Paris, *they're gonna roll right out onto the floor. Then I can squish them good.*

"It's Valentine's Day," someone answered.

"That's right," said Miss Broadnax. "Now, I know you all brought valentines for your friends, and you'll have a chance to exchange those later. But today, we're going to work on a special valentine for your mom."

Which mom is that? thought Paris. *The one in New York City? The one who didn't love Malcolm and me enough to keep us together? The one who liked going out with strangers better than staying at home with her kids? Or the mom who comes to my room every night?*

Paris sighed. *Last Valentine's Day, me and Malcolm made valentines for each other. But this year—*

Paris hated how easily sad thoughts could sneak up on her. One thing she was absolutely, positively not going to do was cry in front of everybody.

"What is it?" asked Ashley, next to her.

"Nothing," said Paris.

"Okay," said Miss Broadnax, "I need a helper to pass out materials. Paris, give me a hand, honey."

Paris loved Miss Broadnax.

Thank you, thank you, thank you, thought Paris. She was happy to be busy so she wouldn't have to think so much. So she wouldn't have to remember.

When the cards were finished, Miss Broadnax collected them all, including the cards students had brought from home. Using one manila envelope per student, she placed every valentine with his or her name on it inside. Later that morning, she called the students up one by one, and handed out the envelopes. That way, no one had to know how many, or how few, valentines everyone else received.

Paris eyed the size of each envelope. Most were a little pudgy, some were stuffed, and a few were fairly flat.

One was thin as a jelly sandwich. Paris figured that one was hers, and she was right.

It doesn't matter, Paris told herself.

At recess, David found her under a stairwell, clutching her manila envelope, her face dirty with tears. She wouldn't tell him what the tears were for. She hardly knew herself.

That evening, when Paris went to her room after dinner, she found an envelope stuffed into her top dresser drawer. The envelope held a splashy red velvet heart, trimmed in silver. Inside were the words, "Happy Valentine's Day, Paris." Paris flipped the card over, hunting for a signature, but there was none. Even so, somehow Paris knew that the card had come from David. It was the same kind of thing Malcolm would have done.

Realizing that warmed Paris from the inside out.

Chapter 20

FAST TRACK

Two sleds. Boys versus girls. Saturday mornings in winter were made for this. Paris was sure of it.

"You know we're gonna beat your butts, right?" said Ashley. "My dad taught me to sled, and my dad is the fastest."

"Talk is cheap," said David. "And you're all talk!"

"Let's just go," said Paris, anxious to get started.

Jordan clutched David's waist, steadying himself for the ride. David gave the word.

"Ready. Set. Go!"

With Ashley steering, she and Paris took off first, getting a good three-foot jump on the boys. Paris felt her heart leap inside her as their sled picked up speed, careening down the steep hill.

"Hold on!" Ashley yelled into the wind, as if Paris needed a reminder. Ashley might well have a tough time peeling Paris off of her once the race was over.

"Whew!" Catching up, the boys came dangerously close to a parked car, then spun out into the intersection, full throttle. Paris looked up in time to see a Jeep bearing down on all of them. The driver swerved, missing both sleds by a hair. Both pairs of racers crashed into the curb and rolled before coming to a complete stop.

For several moments, there was silence. Then, one by one, Paris and the others jumped up, patting themselves to make sure no bones were broken.

Once Jordan knew he wasn't going to die, he broke out laughing. Ashley joined him, then David, then Paris. The air was so cold, every breath they took was visible. Laughing together, the four of them kicked up quite a cloud.

"So, who won?" asked David, wiping tears from his eyes.

Paris and Ashley shrugged. Once that car was coming at them, they'd lost all focus.

"All right," said David. "We'll call it a draw. There's still the park, though. Let's see who's fastest there."

He and Jordan righted their sled and lugged it the few

feet into the park. David picked a strapping maple to mark their new starting point. Paris and Ashley joined the boys there, ready for the next challenge.

They raced down the slope, dragged their sleds uphill, and raced down again too many times to count. They finally stopped when their fannies were sore and the cold drove them to daydreams of hot chocolate.

Frozen as her arms and legs were, Paris had never felt happier.

My friend, she thought, rolling the words around in her mind. *My brothers.*

Paris smiled as the foursome trudged up the hill.

"We're back!" David announced, as the four filed in.

Mrs. Lincoln came to the door. "Hello, Ashley," she said.

"Hi, Mrs. Lincoln."

"Paris," said Mrs. Lincoln, "can I see you for a minute?"

Paris followed her into the dining room.

"While you were out, your mother called. She wants you to visit her in New York next weekend. She's already made the arrangements."

Paris sank into the nearest chair, the winter chill suddenly melting in the heat of her anger.

Ashley came into the room. "Paris?" she said, sensing a change in her friend. "What happened?"

Paris looked up at the girl and shook her head.

You'd never understand, thought Paris. *Not in a million years.*

Chapter 21

THE VISIT

Paris stepped down from the train at Penn Station and slowly made her way to the terminal. Why hurry? It wasn't as if she wanted to be there.

She is your mother, thought Paris, feeling guilty.

So what? I still don't want to see her.

Paris rode the escalator up to the main hall, already longing for the return trip the following day. As soon as she reached the top, she heard her name.

"Paris! Over here," said Viola. "Hi, baby."

Viola bent low to give her daughter a hug. Paris recoiled at her mother's touch, but feeling another wave of guilt, she allowed herself to be held for a moment before wriggling out of her mother's arms.

Viola pretended not to notice. Instead, she grabbed Paris' overnight bag and said, "Let's go home."

Paris coughed, choking on the word.

Home? What is she talking about? She must mean her *home. I don't have a home here anymore,* thought Paris. *Especially not with her.*

Paris kept tight-lipped, following the familiar stranger onto one subway train, then another, and finally up the steps that led to a third-floor walkup on 147th Street and Convent Avenue.

The apartment was clean enough, with no bottles of brandy in sight, but Paris knew they could be hiding in cabinets or dresser drawers. She'd even found one behind the hamper, once.

Give me a few minutes, thought Paris. *If there's a bottle here, I'll find it.*

Viola noticed Paris giving the place the once-over. "I know it's small," she said, misunderstanding.

"Where's my brother?" asked Paris, before she even knew the question was on the tip of her tongue.

Caught off guard, Viola said, "Well, honey, I don't think now is the time to—"

"Where is he?" Paris almost shouted.

"In a group home. At St. Christopher's, in Dobbs Ferry," said Viola.

Dobbs Ferry. Dobbs Ferry. Paris remembered those words. She'd seen them. Where?

"It's a few train stops before Ossining."

"I want to see him," said Paris.

Viola sighed. "All right. I'll make arrangements for sometime soon. But you can't see him today. Now, let me show you around."

Paris nodded stiffly, then dutifully followed her mother around the one-bedroom, railroad-style apartment. A narrow hall ran the length of it, doors on the right and left opening onto a living room, bedroom, kitchen, and bath. Paris looked but didn't really see anything. All her thoughts were on Malcolm.

The day marched by in a most unusual fashion. Viola took Paris out for a lunch of burgers, took her shopping for new boots and sweaters, then made her a dinner of spaghetti and meatballs—her favorite. The food was delicious, and Paris liked her new clothes, but she couldn't help thinking that her mother was trying to make up for missing Christmas, or maybe even trying to buy her love.

It won't work, thought Paris. *I don't love you anymore.*

But even as she thought it, Paris knew it was a lie. She still loved her mother. She just didn't want to. Loving her meant getting hurt, and Paris had had enough of hurting.

. . .

The following day Paris slept in late and woke to the spicy smell of sausage and the sizzle of pancakes in a skillet.

Over breakfast, Viola ventured a question about Ossining: "What's the house like?"

At first, Paris was vague. "Nice. Old, but nice."

"And the family?"

"They're nice."

"I hear they have a dog."

Paris smiled. "Jet. He's as big as a pony. Malcolm would like him."

Viola sighed, shifting in her chair uncomfortably. She tried again.

"Have you made any friends since you've been there?"

Paris thought of Ashley, wondering what her friend was up to that morning.

"There's one," said Paris. "Her name's Ashley. She lives down the street."

"What's she like?"

Paris thought for a moment. How would she describe her new friend?

"She's not like anybody," said Paris. "I mean, she doesn't care what anybody thinks, she's not afraid of anything—she's different. You could tell that right away." Then Paris told her mother about that first day in class, how she'd met Ashley, and how they'd turned out to be neighbors. She described the super Valentine's Day card Ashley'd made for her, and about the great sled race, and before Paris knew it, she and her mother were smiling and laughing together. Paris loved her mother's deep-belly, let-it-all-out laugh. She'd almost forgotten that laugh. And the music. There was always music playing in the house, and suddenly Paris realized where her own love of music came from. She'd gotten more from her mother than her eyes and nose. Paris smiled at the thought, feeling more connected to Viola than ever.

Late that afternoon, Viola took Paris back to Penn Station. Viola escorted Paris onto the train, balancing her overnight case and her extra bags of new clothing. She helped Paris get settled in her seat.

"All aboard!"

It was time to say good-bye, and this time, when Viola hugged Paris, Paris hugged her back.

"See you soon, sweetie," she said, then rushed off the train.

Paris waved to her mother through the window, a sudden flash of sadness blinding her, stinging her eyes, making them wet.

"Good-bye, Mommy."

Chapter 22

HOMECOMING

Paris returned to the welcome routine of school. She slipped into her seat beside Ashley as Miss Broadnax began taking the roll.

"Patti Anderson."

"Here."

"Matt Brooks."

"Here."

"Where were you all weekend?" Ashley whispered.

"Ashley Corbett."

"Shh," said Paris. "I'll tell you later."

"Ashley Corbett!"

"Oh! Here. Mostly."

Paris grinned.

That girl'll say anything.

· · ·

Come lunchtime, Paris had made up her mind to tell Ashley straight out. She might as well. Ashley would probably bug her to death until Paris told her, anyway.

"I went to see my mother—my real mother—in the city."

"Oh!" said Ashley, between bites of her sandwich. "So? How was it?"

Paris considered the best word to use. "It was—weird. At first, I didn't want to see her at all. Then, I was kinda glad to see her again. Then, by the time I left, I was sad to go, but also happy to be coming back here. It's all mixed up in my head."

Ashley nodded as if she understood. Paris knew that she didn't but she could see that her friend was trying, and that counted for something.

"Want some oatmeal cookies?" asked Ashley, after a time. "My mom packed a bunch of extras today."

"Sure," said Paris, happy to return to safer ground. "Hand them over. Mmm, mmm, mmm! Your mom makes the best cookies!" said Paris, licking the crumbs from her fingers.

"My daddy says she's the best cook in seven states!"

"Where is your daddy, anyway?" asked Paris. "I never see him."

"He's a salesman," said Ashley. "Always on the road. You'll meet him, one of these days."

Paris shrugged. It seemed like most of the daddies she knew were ghosts. Why should Ashley's daddy be any different?

"I'm starving, here," said Paris. "I need another cookie. Hurry, or I'll have to call 911!"

Ashley shook her head, and broke the last cookie in half.

Chapter 23

CHOIR PRACTICE

Paris' math workbook was one colossal smudge.

That's what you get for rushing, thought Paris. But she couldn't help herself. According to house rules, unless she finished her homework on time, she couldn't go to choir, and if she didn't get to go to choir, she'd die. No question.

Paris solved the last problem on the page, slammed the workbook on her desk, and grabbed her jacket.

Easter was less than two weeks away, and Star of Bethlehem's choirs were getting ready. The youth choir had two songs to sing: "Christ the Lord Is Risen Today," which they'd sing together with the adult choir, and a punched-up version of "Because He Lives," which would show off all their hard work on three-part harmony. Paris couldn't wait.

"What're you wearing?" asked the girl standing to her right.

"What?"

"On Easter. Did you get your new dress yet?"

Paris shook her head, suddenly concerned.

Briana's right. What am I gonna wear?

Half the kids in the choir had been buzzing about the new clothes their moms had bought them for Easter. New hats, too. Not everyday boots and sweaters like Viola had bought Paris, but patent-leather Mary Janes with bows on them, flouncy taffeta dresses with poofy sleeves for the girls, and navy blue suits with crisp white shirts for the boys. Nobody had taken Paris shopping for those kinds of clothes.

I'm gonna be the only one wearing old clothes, thought Paris. *I'm gonna stick out. Shoot! Why can't we wear robes like the grown-up choir?*

"Good evening!"

The youth choir director tapped the music stand with her baton to get everyone's attention.

"All right, kids. Time to focus. Let's get serious, now. Remember: God is watching." Paris looked up, as if to catch a glimpse of him.

The director led the choir in scales, as a warm-up. Then she tapped the music stand a second time.

"Good! Now turn to 'Because He Lives,' page two hundred thirteen. Although most of you should know the words, by now."

Good thing the music arrangement was up-tempo. Otherwise, Paris would have rocked herself to sleep in its rhythm. As it was, she closed her eyes while she sang so that the words could sink into her.

> *Because he lives, I can face tomorrow.*
> *Because he lives, all fear is gone . . .*

Paris sang the words and they became true for her. She wasn't afraid anymore. Not of being beaten, or being locked in a closet. Not of the dark, or of never seeing Malcolm again, or of nobody wanting her. And she wasn't even afraid of sticking out on Easter. Paris could hardly recognize the fearless person she was turning into.

> *Because I know he holds the future . . .*

She was learning to keep God in her pocket, and because she had him to talk to, she was beginning to have faith that she'd be all right.

Chapter 24

SATURDAY SURPRISE

Saturday morning found Paris playing hide-and-seek with David and Jordan. Jordan was It, which meant that he was hiding in the shed. David and Paris both knew that because it was where Jordan always hid. Either he didn't quite get the game, or he liked being in the shed, they couldn't figure out which. Either way, they took their time "finding" him to stretch the game out.

"I wonder if Jordan's behind this bush," said Paris, loudly. "Nope. Not here."

"Hey! I know," said David. "I'll bet he's in Jet's doghouse!" A giggle came from the shed. That was when Paris pushed the door open.

"Gotcha!" she cried. Still giggling, Jordan stepped out onto the grass. Now, it was Paris' turn. She loved the game. She was better than anyone at hiding. That was the main reason David agreed to play. Paris made it a challenge.

The boys both covered their eyes and started counting to ten.

"One." Paris sprinted toward the house. There were more places to hide inside than there were in the yard.

"Two. Three." Paris opened the screen door gingerly, careful not to let it bang behind her.

"Four. Five—"

"Kids!" called their mother from the living room. "Get in here."

Paris groaned. So much for hide-and-seek.

"David! Jordan! Now!"

The boys joined Paris, wondering how their mom was going to ruin their Saturday fun.

"Wash your hands and get in the car. Jordan, tie your laces before you trip over them."

"Where are we going?" asked David.

"Get in the car and you'll see."

With bottom lips dragging on the floor, Paris and David grumbled and headed out the door.

Paris slouched in the backseat, disinterested in the view out the window. Jordan bounced up and down in the front. He was always excited to go for a drive, no matter where.

David hated being cooped up in a car. To keep himself from going stir-crazy, he counted every black car they passed.

A few minutes later, the car came to a complete stop. Paris looked out the window and saw that they were parked in the center of town.

"Let's go," said Mrs. Lincoln.

The kids piled out and followed her into a clothing store. She waved David and Jordan over to the boys' section.

"Start looking around for a suit you might like for Easter," she said. "I'll be over there to help you in a minute. Go on." Then she turned to Paris.

"As for us, we are going to go find you a dress."

"A dress?" said Paris. "For me?"

"You see any other little girls here?" Mrs. Lincoln read the surprise on Paris' face. "Easter's almost here," she said, "and every Easter, I buy my kids new clothes. You're one of my kids now, Paris. And I treat all my kids the same. I'm taking Earletta shopping next week. So, come on. Let's find you a dress."

Paris nodded, the lump in her throat making it impossible to speak.

For the next hour, Paris tried on nearly every dress in her size. She ran her fingers over yards of silk, nylon, dotted swiss, and sheer cotton. She pulled the last dress over her head. It was a beautiful sea-foam green and picked up the flecks of green in her hazel eyes. She didn't even like dresses, but she loved this one.

Paris stared at her new self in the mirror. She couldn't help wondering how long this all would last. How long she'd get to be one of Mrs. Lincoln's kids.

She closed her eyes and shook off the thought, turning her imagination to her next choir practice.

Just wait, she thought. *I'll get to brag about my new Easter clothes like everybody else.*

This thought made her smile inside and out.

"I like this one," said Paris.

"Well then," said Mrs. Lincoln, "it's yours."

Chapter 25

WORD

For once, Viola kept her word.

She made arrangements for the two of them to visit Malcolm. She had Paris take the train down to Dobbs Ferry and met her at the station. A short taxi ride later, and mother and daughter were on the grounds of St. Christopher's Home for Children.

An attendant directed them to the visitors' lounge, then sent word to Malcolm's housemother that they had arrived.

Paris sat on the edge of a chair, drumming her thighs anxiously as she waited. The minute Malcolm crossed the threshold of the entryway, Paris flew into his arms. They stood right there, holding each other until other visitors were forced to squeeze by.

Malcolm looked over his sister's shoulder and nodded hello to Viola. She nodded back.

"Go on," she said, motioning toward the door that led to a small picnic area. "I'll join you two later."

Hand in hand, brother and sister walked into the sunshine. They found a table cloaked in shade, and sat opposite one another.

Paris kept staring at her brother to make sure she wasn't dreaming. "I missed you, Malcolm," said Paris.

"I missed you, too, squirt."

Paris wore a smile bright as a Fourth of July sparkler at first, but the smile faded as she noticed a hardness in her brother's face that hadn't been there before.

"How are you, Malcolm?" Paris asked.

Malcolm shrugged, lowering his eyes. "I'm okay," he said. "It's not so bad here." His voice told Paris something different. "The room I stay in is kind of crowded. There are three other guys in it besides me." He shrugged again. "It could be worse. I'll tell you one thing, though. The food here stinks!"

They both laughed at that. Paris and Malcolm had shared some pretty awful meals together at the Boones'. Not to mention those disasters Malcolm tried to make for the two of them when Viola was AWOL, back in the city.

Once, Malcolm had dished up some uncooked oatmeal with buttermilk. Yuck!

"Forget about me," said Malcolm. "Tell me about you."

And so Paris told him. About the house on the hill. About Jet. About Ashley. About school. About how she tricked the psychologist with that stupid inkblot test. About the choir. About her Easter dress. She even told him about the letters she wrote to him when she first got to Ossining.

Paris rambled on and on and didn't stop until she saw something in her brother's face break open. She watched as the beginnings of a familiar smile took shape.

"What is it?" asked Paris.

"He listened," whispered Malcolm.

"Who?"

"God," said Malcolm, looking up. "I bugged him, every single day since I got here, I bugged him to look out for you, to take care of my little sister. And he listened."

Paris and Malcolm locked eyes. She was relieved to see a bit of the old Malcolm shining through. She reached across the table and took her brother's hand.

"You've just got to keep God in your pocket, and everything will be all right," said Paris.

"What?"

Paris pursed her lips, trying to figure out how to explain what she meant. "Put your hands in your pockets," she said.

"Paris—"

"Go on."

"Okay. Now what?"

"Pretend that God is there. See? You stick your hand in your pocket, and remind yourself that God's always close by, and you can talk to him whenever you need to," said Paris.

Malcolm nodded. "I get it. Keep God in your pocket. Cool," he said. "I'll give that a try. Thanks, little sister."

"You're welcome," said Paris. "But I'm not so little anymore."

Malcolm threw his head back and laughed. "You got that right!"

"What's so funny?" asked Viola, joining them at last.

"Nothing," they said in unison.

"You two can't fool me. You've got that look, like you've been sharing deep, dark secrets. I've seen that look before. You're up to something."

Paris and Malcolm grinned at each other. They liked being up to something good.

Chapter 26

EASTER SUNDAY

Paris tried her best not to let on how excited she was about Easter, but when the day rolled around, she used up every drop of hot water in the house to take a shower that went on forever. She even washed behind her ears, twice, without being told. When she was sure God himself could not have found a speck of dirt on her, she toweled off and hurried to her bedroom to dress.

She'd chosen the right dress, no doubt about it. But Paris frowned at her reflection in the mirror. She'd have to do something with her hair. Maybe Mrs. Lincoln could help. Paris went down to the master bedroom and knocked on the door.

"Hold on," said Mr. Lincoln. A few seconds later, he opened the door a crack.

"Morning, Paris. Oh! I see you're dressed already. I'm moving kind of slow, myself."

"I need to see Mom," Paris blurted out.

"I think she left early, dear. She said something about helping to set the doughnuts out, and getting the coffee started. You can check—" Paris never heard the rest.

Not ready to give up, she ran to Earletta's room and knocked.

"Is Mom in there?" she called through the door.

"No, Mom is not in here!" snapped Earletta, clearly annoyed.

After a long pause, Paris asked, "Are you sure?"

Earletta stuck her head out the door and studied Paris carefully. The girl looked miserable.

"Why're you looking for Mom?"

Paris grabbed a hank of hair and held it away from her scalp. "This," she said. "I don't know what to do with it."

Most days, Paris simply pulled her hair back in a ponytail. But today was special, and she wanted her hair to be special, too.

Earletta sighed, opening her door wider. "Come in and sit down," she said. "Not on my bed! On the chair."

Paris did as she was told, awed by the invitation into Earletta's private world. Earletta never let anyone in there.

"Are you tender-headed?" asked Earletta.

Paris shook her head no.

"All right, then. Sit still."

Earletta ran a comb through Paris' hair first, pulling out the tangles. Then she brushed it front to back, in a slow, easy rhythm that almost put Paris to sleep.

"Just as well you came to me, anyway," said Earletta. "Mom's no good at hair, in case you haven't figured that out already. She's used to boys. I should know. I was the first girl in this house. They had four foster kids before me—all boys."

No wonder, thought Paris. *That's why Mom lets me do my own hair. She doesn't know how.*

"Be right back," said Earletta, handing the brush to Paris. She left the room and came back a minute later holding a length of sea-foam green ribbon, the same color as Paris' dress.

What's she going to do with that? Paris wondered.

"Okay. Hold your head still," said Earletta.

Paris braced herself against the back of the chair until Earletta was done. When she was finished, Earletta gave Paris a hand mirror. "Go look in the full-length mirror on the back of my door," she said. "That way, you can see how your hair looks in the back."

What Paris saw was a perfect French braid, every single hair tucked in place, with the length of ribbon woven through it. Paris squealed, dropped the mirror on the bed, and threw her arms around Earletta's waist.

"Thankyouthankyouthankyouthankyou!" said Paris.

"Get off me, girl," said Earletta, pushing Paris away. But Paris noticed that Earletta's voice was softer than her words. "I've got to get ready for church, too, you know."

Paris backed away, smiling, and left the room feeling ready for her big day.

Mr. Lincoln finished dressing, then drove them all to church. Paris stood on the front steps awhile, turning her head this way and that to make sure everyone noticed her French braid. Then she realized Mrs. Lincoln hadn't seen her all dressed up, so Paris hurried to the church dining room in the basement to find her. Mrs. Lincoln wasn't one to ooh and ahh, but when she saw Paris, she gave a nod of approval and said, "Nice. Very nice." Paris stood there preening until she heard the organ music, which reminded her that it was time to join the choir lining up outside of the sanctuary, preparing to march in.

The youth choir marched in first, their faces gleaming like star-shine. The congregation was on its feet, a sway-ing rainbow of yellow and hot pink, turquoise and royal blue, peach and purple, and, here and there, a shot of or-ange. Then there were the flowers! There were as many on hat bands, it seemed, as there were lilies adorning the altar.

Once in place, the combined choirs opened with "Were You There?" then moved on to "Christ the Lord Is Risen Today." All the voices of the congregation rose, too. Easter arrived at Star of Bethlehem with a shout.

The pastor came forward and led the church in prayer. Then the Scripture was read, and the pastor announced the title of his sermon: The flip side of the Crucifixion.

That was about all Paris heard. After that, her mind was busy running over the lines of her song, her first-ever solo. The last thing she wanted was to mess it up. If that happened, Paris knew she would absolutely die!

Before Paris knew it, the adult choir director was nodding toward her. She looked back at him, confused, until he waved her forward, motioning toward the microphone. In that very moment, Paris went blank.

Her feet were rooted to the floor. She couldn't move.

Oh no, oh no, oh no, oh no, oh no! thought Paris. Her heart beat wildly against her rib cage. Every particle of air left the room. Paris thought she would faint.

Then she heard a voice whisper, *It's all right, Paris. Calm down.*

Malcolm? thought Paris. She couldn't be sure. But she felt her heartbeat slow. She took a deep breath and felt a little stronger. She smoothed the skirt of her dress, feeling for a pocket that wasn't there. Paris started to panic again, but then she remembered. *It's pretend,* she told herself. And she closed her eyes, slipped her hand into her pretend pocket, and reminded herself that God was near, as close as her hand in her pocket.

Paris looked up at the congregation and walked calmly to the microphone. She stood straight, opened her mouth, and found the words of the song there, waiting for her. Paris sang.

The next thing she knew, the congregation was on its feet, applauding.

After the service, people kept coming up to her and saying things like, "Child, the Lord sure did bless you with a voice!" and "You keep on singing, baby. God bless you!" Even Earletta came up to Paris and whispered in her ear, "You were the best one up there."

The whole while, David stuck close, slinging his arm across her shoulders.

"She sure can sing, can't she?" said David. "And you know why? Because talent runs in the family. I told you she's my sister, right?"

"Mine, too!" piped up Jordan.

Paris couldn't stop grinning.

Chapter 27

THE PHOTOGRAPH

Easter break was over, and it was back to school for Paris.

One afternoon, when she had finished her homework, she padded downstairs to see what everyone else was up to. Mrs. Lincoln was in her easy chair with a photo album spread open across her ample lap. A bottle of glue and stacks of snapshots sat on a table tray nearby.

"Oh! Perfect! You're here," said Mrs. Lincoln, when Paris entered the room. "You can help me out with these," she said, handing Paris an envelope of photographs. "Look through these and pick out your favorite."

"Huh?" said Paris, turning the envelope over in her hand.

"Pick out your favorite picture so that I can make sure

to add it to the album. I've already picked a few. Now it's your turn."

"Okay," said Paris, perplexed. She couldn't figure out why her opinion of the photographs mattered. It wasn't like they were *her* photographs, right?

Paris had seen very few pictures of herself. Ever. There'd been a couple of baby pictures, but that was about it. Viola wasn't much into taking pictures, and the Boones never bothered taking any of her. They'd concentrated on taking pictures of their own kids.

Paris slipped the black-and-white prints out of the envelope and flipped through them quickly. A smile of surprise and gratitude inched its way across her face. The photographs were of Easter Sunday, and every one of them included Paris. They were all candid shots, and Paris had never known they were being taken.

Paris turned to Mrs. Lincoln and opened her mouth to say something, but no words came out. Mrs. Lincoln coughed and looked away, as she often did when she was uncomfortable with emotion.

"Well, go on," she said, in a gruff voice. "Pick out the one you like best and give it here."

Paris turned back to the small stack of photos and studied them closely, now. One was of her at the front of the church, belting out her solo. Another was of her and David. He had his arm slung across her shoulders, and he was beaming proudly. Paris grinned. *That's when he told everybody I was his sister,* she remembered. There were a few shots with Earletta in the background, by herself or standing with her high school friends. There were other photos of Paris singing with the choir, one of her straightening Jordan's tie, and another of her smoothing the skirt of her brand-new dress when she thought nobody was looking. Then there was a shot of the three of them, David and Paris and Jordan, smiling together on the church steps before they went inside. Paris beamed.

"This is the one," Paris said, handing that last photo to Mrs. Lincoln.

"Okay!" said Mrs. Lincoln, a few minutes later. "All done." She closed the album and asked Paris to set it on the coffee table.

"Can I look at it first?" Paris asked.

"Sure," said Mrs. Lincoln. "Just put it back on the coffee table when you're done."

Paris carried the leather-bound book to the dining room, away from the racket of the television so she could enjoy the album in relative quiet.

As she turned the pages, she found people she knew, and people she didn't. There were photos of aunts and uncles and cousins she'd met at Thanksgiving and Christmas. There were shots of men at Con Edison who worked with Mr. Lincoln. Paris figured out who they were because they all wore shirts with the company logo. And there were shots of David and Jordan, and even a few of Earletta. And now, there were several shots of Paris, including a new one of her singing, and the one she had chosen herself, and that made her happy. Almost.

One thing bothered her. All of the Lincolns, including the aunts and uncles and cousins, looked alike. You could tell they were related. And when you looked at pictures of David and Jordan, it was clear they belonged to each other. Earletta was the same color as the Lincolns, at least. But not Paris. She didn't look like any of them, in any way. And why should she? This wasn't her family, not really. These weren't pictures of *her* aunts and uncles, of *her* cousins. The eyes and ears that stared back at Paris from the mirror every morning were different from the ones that stared back at her from these photographs. If she wanted to find her features, she'd have to stare into the face of her birth mother, Viola.

Paris ran her fingers over the photo of the Lincoln boys and herself. She returned the album to the coffee table and went to her room. But first, Paris called Viola and asked if she had any family pictures she could send.

Chapter 28

A TIME TO WEED

March melted into April, and the weather began to warm.

"Time to weed the flower beds," said Mrs. Lincoln one Saturday over breakfast. "Who wants to help?"

Mr. Lincoln was sleeping in, for a change. The boys kept munching their cereal. Earletta popped her last forkful of eggs into her mouth, cleared her plate from the table, and left the kitchen.

Lazybones, thought Paris. Of course, Paris had no idea what weeding flower beds entailed. She'd had little experience with yards and flower beds in New York City.

"I'll help," she said. David and Jordan exchanged looks, shaking their heads.

"See you next year," David muttered. Jordan giggled.

"What?" asked Paris. *"What?"*

· · ·

Once Paris looked at it closely, she could see that the entire backyard was a hopscotch of dandelions and clover. She'd be pulling weeds forever! No wonder nobody else wanted the job.

Should've kept my big mouth shut, thought Paris. But at least she was outdoors. And she was looking forward to seeing the garden in full bloom. It wouldn't kill her to help the garden get that way, now would it?

Paris set to work around the hydrangeas. She used a small spade to break the ground and loosen it up like Mrs. Lincoln told her, so she could yank the weeds, root and all.

The soil was teeming with critters. Paris had to shake off ants several times, and more than once disturbed an earthworm who didn't appreciate being exposed to the sun.

How do they see down there? Paris wondered. *And look how fast they move!*

Fascinated, Paris was doing more watching than weeding. If she hadn't, she'd never have seen the snake.

"It won't hurt you," said David, suddenly behind her. "Garter snakes aren't poisonous."

That was all Paris needed to hear. "Good," she said. "I think I'll keep it, then."

"I don't know about that," said David. But Paris had already picked the small snake up, and before he knew it, she'd run into the house to show off her new pet. David and Jordan ran in after her.

"Mom! Mom! Look what I found!" called Paris, banging into the house. "Mom, where are you?"

"In the living room."

Paris bounded into the room, shoes muddy from the spring-wet ground.

"Mom, look!" She shoved the snake under Mrs. Lincoln's nose. Mrs. Lincoln gasped, her eyes nearly crossing.

"Get that thing out of here," she said in a clipped and dangerous voice.

"But, Mom," said Paris, inching even closer, "it's a garter snake. See?"

"Out!" ordered Mrs. Lincoln. "Now!"

Behind her, Paris could hear muffled laughter. As she retraced her muddy steps, the boys stumbled a few feet ahead of her, doubled over with laughter.

"That was funny!" David said, once they were back outside.

Paris felt her jaw tighten. Mrs. Lincoln had all but taken her head off. Paris was in no mood for laughter. Worst of all, she didn't even know what she'd done wrong.

"Mom's scared of snakes," explained Jordan.

"Can't stand 'em," added David.

"Well, you could've told me," snapped Paris, returning the snake to the soil.

"I didn't get a chance," said David. He had to wipe tears from his eyes. "Besides, I'm glad I didn't. Man, did you see the look on her face? I thought her eyes were gonna pop right out of her head!" David erupted in laughter again, and this time, Paris joined him.

Imagine, thought Paris. *Mom being afraid of something, of* anything, *least of all a little old snake.* Somehow, the thought of it made Paris love her more.

Chapter 29

THE GREAT ESCAPE

First a snake, then a bird. God's creatures made life interesting in the Lincoln home that spring.

One day, after endless begging from Jordan, Mr. Lincoln bought the family a parakeet. Jordan named the bird Feathers, and the first time it was Jordan's turn to clean the cage, Feathers escaped.

Paris spotted the runaway bird when it nearly clipped her flying low through the kitchen where Paris was munching on a sandwich.

"Whoa!" said Paris. "Jordan! What's this bird doing out of his cage?"

"Yikes!" said David, ducking down as Feathers buzzed through the living room.

"David! Jordan! Somebody get that bird back in its

cage!" orderd Mrs. Lincoln. "Lord knows, I'm too old to be chasing that bird around the house."

Feathers flew to the second floor with David in pursuit. Jordan met him at the top of the landing, and they both chased the bird into Earletta's room.

"I got him! I got him!" said Jordan, reaching for the bird, now perched on Earletta's dresser. But Feathers took off again, flapping his way back into the hall.

Paris went upstairs to join the chase.

"Come here, Feathers," she cooed. "That's a nice bird."

"Here, Feathers," called Jordan. "Come on, little birdy."

Mrs. Lincoln called upstairs, "Don't come down here until that bird is back in its cage!"

"You making any progress?" asked Mr. Lincoln, lumbering up the stairs.

"Not yet," said David.

Mr. Lincoln started whistling, which brought the bird flying in his direction. He reached out to capture the wily bird, but missed. Those near-misses went on for an hour.

Finally, the bird settled on the desk in Paris' room.

"Stay back," Paris whispered. "I'll get him. Just be quiet."

Very, very slowly, Paris tiptoed into her room, went

to her desk, and sat down. Keeping one eye on the parakeet, she reached down for the wicker basket next to her desk, and with one swift motion, brought the basket down over the bird. A few minutes later, Feathers was back in his cage.

Paris went downstairs to watch TV. When she entered the living room, Mr. Lincoln looked up.

"Good job," he told Paris. "Maybe we should start calling you the Big Bad Bird-catcher of Ossining! What do you think?"

The very idea made Paris giggle.

Chapter 30

FAMILY PORTRAIT

The night before her birthday, Paris went to her room and took out the photo of Malcolm and Viola and herself that she'd received one week after calling her birth mother. She was barely two years old in that picture, so she didn't remember it being taken.

On the back of the photo, Viola had written "Three peas." Paris smiled. Her mother always used to say the three of them looked so similar, they were like three peas in a pod.

Paris stared at the picture for a long time. Those faces told Paris there would always be someone in this world she belonged to, even if it wasn't the Lincolns. Trouble was, part of her wanted to belong to them as well. Was that wrong?

"Don't get too comfortable," Earletta had warned Paris when she first arrived. "You probably won't be here that long."

But Paris had been with the Lincolns for nearly one whole school year. They'd nestled into a corner of her heart, and she'd learned that she could trust them. So maybe it was okay to start thinking of their family as her own.

Still, Paris ached for Malcolm. There were even times when she missed Viola.

I wish there were two of me, thought Paris. *That way, both of us could have the family we want.*

Chapter 31

MAY 24

Dear Malcolm,

Thanks for my birthday card. I was afraid nobody would re-member, like last year when we were at the Boone's.

This year was better.

Today, I got off from doing chores. I didn't even have to make my bed! But I made it anyway. (You know me.) I got a card from David and Jordan, and Earletta took me shopping at the 99-cent store and told me to buy whatever I wanted. I picked out a puzzle cause it made me think of you.

You got any puzzles, there?

After dinner, Mom Lincoln set a big ole ice cream cake right in front of me, and everybody sang Happy Birthday. Earletta said Mom Lincoln always finds out the birthday of every foster kid when they get here, then writes it in a book so she won't forget.

Do they have birthday parties for the kids where you are? I hope so.

I gotta go.

Love, Paris

Chapter 32

THE INTRODUCTION

The first hot breath of late spring blew the chill from Riverview Road. No one who was home bothered closing their front door. So when Paris stepped onto Ashley's porch one afternoon, all that separated her from whoever sat in the living room was a thin sheet of screen. Paris rang the doorbell.

"Charlotte," came a man's voice, "get the door."

Ashley's dad! thought Paris. *It must be. Now I'm finally going to meet him.*

"What the hell is a little blonde-headed nigger girl doing darkening the door of my house?"

The slap of words knocked Paris back two feet. Before she could catch her breath, Ashley's mother was at the door.

Speaking in a voice loud enough to carry through the house, Mrs. Corbett said, "I told you yesterday, we don't buy cookies at this house. We make our own." Then, in a voice close to a whisper, she said, "This is not a good time, Paris. Go home."

Cookies? thought Paris. *What is she talking about?*

"But, Mrs. Corbett," Paris began. "I don't—"

"Go home, Paris!" Mrs. Corbett whispered. "Ashley Marie can't play with you. I'm sorry. Now go on home."

In a louder voice, she said, "And don't come back!" With that, Mrs. Corbett slammed the door, and as she did, Paris caught a glimpse of Ashley hanging back in her mother's shadow.

Paris retraced the steps to her house on wooden legs. She sat on the porch swing for a long time, trying to take in what had just happened. But like a stone skipped on water, the pain of it sent ripples of hurt throughout her mind and body, and Paris found it impossible to think. Instead, she stuck her right hand inside her pocket, and without knowing that she did so, she opened her mouth and began to sing.

Jesus loves me, this I know
for the Bible tells me so . . .

As Paris sang, tears rolled down her cheeks.

That was the last day Paris ever asked Ashley to come out and play, and the last time Ashley would dare to call Paris her friend.

Later that afternoon, Paris told Mrs. Lincoln what had happened, and once again, her eyes brimmed with tears. Mrs. Lincoln, who rarely gave hugs, pulled Paris into her arms.

"I'm sorry you had to hear such words," she said. "But that's the way of the world, I'm afraid. There are hateful people in it, Paris, and some of them are white."

"I'll never have another white friend," Paris vowed.

"Don't say that," said Mrs. Lincoln. "You can't go through life judging people by the color of their skin."

"But that's what Ashley's father did!"

"Yes, honey. And he was wrong."

Paris couldn't argue with that. "Then what am I supposed to do?"

"Take each person as they come," said Mrs. Lincoln. "Judge them by their actions. Then decide whether to hold them close or push them away. That's what you do."

Paris listened carefully to Mrs. Lincoln's words. She tucked them away for further consideration, and rested her head on the woman's chest.

The remaining hours of the weekend limped along, dragging Paris with them. She tried to stay out back during the day to avoid running into Ashley. But on Monday morning, they all but collided in the doorway of their classroom.

Paris half expected Ashley to drop her eyes and back away, too embarrassed to make eye contact. Instead, she looked longingly at Paris with eyes that said, "I'm sorry." But Ashley seemed to have lost her voice.

"I was your friend," said Paris, meeting Ashley's gaze. "You should have told your father that." Paris had nothing more to say, but as Ashley squeezed past her, Paris did notice that Ashley didn't stand as straight and proud as she used to. Shame had shriveled her, somehow.

Good, thought Paris. *She should be ashamed.* That was the last thought she spent on Ashley for a long time.

All that truly lifted Paris' spirits after that horrible breakup was getting ready for her choir's next concert. The director had picked Paris for another solo, and she went around the house singing all day, determined to master each note.

Singing was better than thinking, so Paris sang.

Chapter 33

GONE FISHING

The worst thing about little brothers—well, not the worst thing, but one of them—was that they sometimes needed looking after, and Paris was not always in the mood. Her teacher had saddled her with homework and Paris was anxious to get it done so she could enjoy the rest of the afternoon.

"Paris," Mrs. Lincoln called up to her. "Go with Jordan to the park for a little while. He wants to catch a tadpole for show-and-tell, and I don't want him falling in the water."

"Why can't David take him?" Paris asked.

"David's got baseball practice. Besides, I asked *you*."

Paris groaned. "But what about my homework?"

"Finish it later. There's plenty of time before dinner."

Oh well, thought Paris. *It was worth a try.* Out of excuses, she set her spelling list aside and stomped downstairs.

"Come on, Jordan," she called.

Jordan came running, happy to get his wish. Outside, he tried to run ahead of Paris, but she had a death grip on his hand. She wasn't about to get into trouble for letting him run out into the street. Once they reached the park at the foot of the hill, she dropped his hand.

"Be careful with that jar, Jordan," said Paris. "If you break it, you won't have a home for your tadpole."

"Okay," said Jordan. He kneeled by the brook, and began searching the water. A couple of times he thought he had something, but it turned out to be a rock, glistening in the sunlight. This was going to take a while.

There was a park bench nearby, but a pale, freckle-faced girl with a shock of red hair sat on one end of it. Paris sat at the other end, planning to ignore the girl.

Another white girl, thought Paris. No surprise. Except for the Lincolns and two other families, everyone in the neighborhood was white. It was the same at school. Paris was the only black kid in her grade.

In Ossining, if Paris saw more than two or three black faces at one time, it was at church, and few of the kids at Star of Bethlehem went to Claremont. She was friendly with a couple of the kids in the choir, but she only saw them once a week. So, Paris realized, if she was ever going to have any friends on her block, or in her school, likely as not they'd be white. But she sure wasn't shopping around for one. Not after Ashley.

Paris swung her legs over the side of the bench, wondering how long it was going to take for Jordan to find his stupid tadpole.

"Find one yet?" she called to him. Jordan shook his head from side to side.

"What's he looking for?" asked the freckled girl.

"Tadpoles," said Paris. "For school, you know. Show-and-tell."

The girl nodded. With her chin, she pointed to a little boy a few feet away. "Stick insects. Same thing. Show-and-tell. I'll be glad when he's big enough to come to the park on his own."

Paris looked at Jordan and thought, *Me, too,* but she didn't say it.

"I'm Sienna. Sienna Warren. And that's P. J. We just moved here."

Who asked you? thought Paris. Still, she didn't want to be rude.

"I'm Paris, and that's Jordan," she said, hoping that would be the end of it.

But Sienna launched into a series of questions: Where do you live? How old are you? What school do you go to? Paris answered each question, thinking it would be the last. When she could see it wasn't, Paris stood up, called for Jordan, and told him it was time to go. Luckily for Paris, he'd finally caught his tadpole and was ready to leave.

Their exit was anything but speedy, though. Jordan held his tadpole jar with both hands, careful not to drop it, as he inched toward Paris.

Ugh! thought Paris, who couldn't get out of that park fast enough. *Little brothers. What a pain!*

"See you later!" called Sienna. "Maybe at school!"

Paris shook her head and kept walking.

Some folks can't take a hint.

Chapter 34

ME AND MY SHADOW

The following Monday, Paris was sitting in the school lunchroom, eating her tuna salad sandwich, when Sienna slipped into the empty space beside her.

"Hi!" said Sienna, grinning. "I saw you here all by yourself and figured I'd keep you company. You mind?"

You again, thought Paris, her mouth too full to speak. She finished chewing, swallowed, and was about to say she'd rather be alone, when Sienna launched right into a story before Paris could get a word in.

Paris sighed, shaking her head. *Go on, Miss Freckles,* she thought. *Jabber all you want to. I'm not listening.* So Sienna talked enough for the both of them, and Paris finished her lunch in silence, nodding every now and then to keep Sienna from bugging her with questions.

. . .

The week closed with a parent-teacher buffet. The principal called it the last meet-and-greet of the school year, a chance for parents, teachers, and students to celebrate the end of the year.

Mr. and Mrs. Lincoln were there with David, Jordan, and Paris. The minute they got there, David took off looking for his buddies, dragging Jordan behind him. Mr. and Mrs. Lincoln chatted with a couple of teachers, and Paris stood nearby, sipping lemonade by herself.

From the corner of her eye, Paris noticed Sienna hurrying in her direction. Rushing to keep up was a tall man with the same shock of red hair as Sienna, and an equally tall lady who was blonde.

Must be Mr. and Mrs. Freckles, thought Paris. *What do they want?*

"Hi, Paris!" said Sienna, bubbly as a cold root beer. "And Mr. Lincoln, Mrs. Lincoln, right? This is my mom and dad."

"I'm Jake," said Mr. Warren. "And this is my wife, Kendra."

"James and Esther," said Mr. Lincoln. The adults shook hands all around.

Then Mr. Warren bent down until he was his daughter's height.

142

"Hi there! You must be Paris," he said, holding out his hand. Paris looked at it, hesitating. She searched his face, his eyes, and found not an ounce of hatred. Slowly, Paris slid her small hand into his big paw. He gave her hand a warm shake, then stood up.

"Sienna tells me she hopes the two of you are going to be good friends, so it's nice to finally meet you," he said. "And your parents."

Paris glanced up at Mrs. Lincoln, who gave her a secret wink. Paris nodded, turning to Sienna. The girl's smile had faded a little. She looked as if she might be holding her breath.

Good friends, huh? thought Paris. *I don't know.*

The adults chatted with one another while Paris thought, long and hard. She thought about the world of hurt Ashley had caused her. Then she thought about what Mrs. Lincoln had said. *Take every person as she comes. Judge each one by her actions.*

So far, Sienna's actions had been fine, surprising as a spring rain, maybe, but just as soft, too.

Paris polished off her lemonade and headed back to the refreshment table across the room. Midway, she stopped and turned around.

"Well, you coming or not?" she said to Sienna. "I'm about to die of thirst here."

Sienna's smile curved as wide and bright as a crescent moon. She bolted from her father's side and caught up with her friend.

The two girls wandered around together for the rest of the evening.

Chapter 35

PHONE CALL

A lot can happen in a year. Life can become normal, an address can become more than numbers on a piece of paper, and family can become more than just a word in the dictionary.

Paris woke to the honeyed scent of lilacs wafting through her window. Her bedroom was tiny as ever, but the room seemed friendlier. It was no longer a strange place. It was hers. The room, the house, everyone under its roof, and even the scent of lilacs. All were hers, now.

Viola was also hers, but in an arm's-length sort of way. Her birth mother had her life in the city, and Paris had her life in Ossining. She and Malcolm stayed connected through letters mostly. She wished that they were still together, but she was old enough to understand that wasn't a decision she got to make.

"Get up, lazybones," Paris told herself. "Or you'll be late for the last week of school." She rolled out of bed and got ready for the day.

The hours swam by, caught in the current of the ordinary: class, lunch with Sienna, and the noisy car ride home with David play-punching her in the backseat. Before Paris could blink, it was dinnertime and her turn to lay out the knives and forks.

Paris made a detour to the backyard. She clipped a few lilacs for the table and propped them up in a jelly jar full of water. The dash of color was exactly what the table needed.

Dinner was spaghetti and meatballs, her favorite. She couldn't wait to dig in. First, though, she had to bow her head while Mr. Lincoln said grace. Jordan kicked her under the table, being his usual pest of a little brother. Paris didn't give him away, but if looks could kill, let's just say her eyes were busy doing damage during that prayer.

"Amen," said Mr. Lincoln in his deep voice.

Mrs. Lincoln spooned up the spaghetti while Paris retrieved the hot garlic bread from the oven. She was salivating by the time she finally settled back into her seat, and dove into the mountain of spaghetti on her plate. That was when the phone rang. It was Viola. Paris took a bite of garlic bread, then went to the phone.

"Hi," she said. Paris hadn't heard from Viola in a long time, but she was okay with that. She'd given up being angry with her mom, or she'd be mad all the time, and what good would that do?

"Hello, sweetheart! How are you?"

"Fine," said Paris. "But we're eating dinner, Mom."

"I know, I know," said Viola. "And I know I haven't called in a while, and I'm sorry. But I have something important to tell you."

Paris felt her throat tighten. "Is it Malcolm? Is something wrong?"

"No! No, Malcolm's fine," Viola assured her. "But I *am* calling about Malcolm. And about you. And about me. It's something I've been working on for a while, for all of us, honey."

"What is it?" asked Paris, becoming impatient.

"I've gotten married again! His name is Marcus, and he can't wait to meet you. And Malcolm, of course."

"That's nice," said Paris, "but what's that got to do with—"

Viola cut her off. "We've got a great big apartment in Brooklyn, and I've been working hard to get your rooms ready for you. Isn't that great?" Her words ran together.

"We can all be a family again, honey! You and Malcolm can move back to the city, and live with Marcus and me. For good this time. No more foster homes, I promise! Prospect Park is right up the street, and there's a school nearby, I've checked, and I'm sure you'll like it, and the apartment is huge! Did I say that already? I probably did, I'm so excited. The thing is, now that I've straightened myself out, I really want you kids home with me. All you have to do is say yes, honey. If you want."

Viola finally ran out of breath. She fell silent on the other end of the phone.

Paris was stunned.

After all this time, thought Paris. *After all this time.*

I'm just supposed to drop everything and leave Ossining? Leave David, Jordan, and Earletta? Give up my choir, my friends? Give up Mom and Dad Lincoln?

I guess Earletta was right, after all. She's the one kid who gets to stay.

Paris slid to the floor, leaning her full weight against the kitchen cabinet.

The phone cord swung out from the wall and sent the handset banging loudly against the doorjamb.

"Hello? Hello? Are you still there?" said the tinny voice on the phone.

"Paris, what's the matter?" asked Mr. Lincoln.

"Oh, Lord, what did that woman say to her? James, help her up," Mrs. Lincoln said to Mr. Lincoln.

"Hey, Sis. Stop fooling around and get up," said Jordan.

"Yeah," said David.

Paris looked over at her foster family. They were all speaking at once. She could tell because she saw their mouths moving. But for some reason, her ears weren't working. Paris couldn't hear a thing.

For Paris, the rest of the evening was a blur. In a way, that was a special kind of blessing.

Chapter 36

THE GAMBLE

The next morning, for the first time ever, a grown-up asked Paris what she thought.

"The decision is up to you," said Mrs. Lincoln. "If you want to move back to the city and live with your mother, we'll understand. But you know, you'll always have a home here, if you want it, Paris. This time, you choose," she said. Then she left Paris sitting on the edge of her bed, alone.

Choose what? thought Paris. *How? The caseworker says I'm lucky, that most kids don't have a mother who wants them back. Plus, I'd get to live with Malcolm again. But how can I feel lucky? If I go back to the city, that means leaving here. And this is home, now.*

And what about this new stepdad? What if she didn't

like him? What if he didn't like her? And what if she did turn her mother's offer down—what would that mean? Would Viola be out of her life for good? Did she want that? And what if it meant never seeing Malcolm again? Could she risk that?

Paris fell back on the bed and curled up into a ball. She stayed that way for a long time, rocking herself and thinking.

Jet padded into the room and lay at the foot of her bed. Somehow, he knew she needed the company.

The light in the room shifted as noon approached. Paris sat up and looked around. She eyed the wardrobe, the small desk and chair, as well as the night-light on the wall near the door, and she sighed.

"Come here, Jet," she called to the collie. He barked and clambered onto the bed beside her. Paris stroked his back, and let him lick her face.

"Oof!" she said. "You need a bath!" But she didn't push the dog away. Instead, she laid her head against his hairy body and snuggled.

Somehow, Paris made it through that day, and the next, and the one after that.

She had a lot to think about. Like how much she'd come to love the Lincolns. How she'd come to trust them, and to trust herself simply by being around them. And how close she felt to David and Jordan, and sometimes even Earletta. And she thought about Jolene's comment about her not being a real member of the Lincoln family. In the pit of her, Paris knew it was true. Somehow, she'd always be an outsider. Could the Lincolns' love change that?

Then Paris thought about Malcolm and Viola. She thought about how great it would be to live with Malcolm again. And with Viola, whom she'd finally learned to forgive. She thought about how she hardly knew her own mother, really. And she wanted to. She needed to. It'd be a shame to keep her a stranger.

Paris didn't know anything about her mom's new husband, what was it Mom Lincoln had told her? *Judge each person by his own actions.* Paris understood what that meant. She'd have to give this Marcus guy a chance. She'd keep her eye on him, though. And so would Malcolm.

The caseworker says he's nice, thought Paris. *Maybe he is.*

Paris spent a lot of time gazing at the photo of herself sitting on Viola's lap beside Malcolm. She traced the brows, the chins, the dimpled cheeks that they all shared. And when she went to sleep each night, she prayed, asking God to tell her what to do.

By the end of the week, Paris had made her decision.

Chapter 37

DESTINATIONS UNLIMITED

Paris waved to the Lincolns through the train window, tears streaming down her cheek. She'd miss them more than sunshine, but she was wrapped up in their love, and she was taking it with her.

Tarrytown, Dobbs Ferry, Riverdale. As Paris got closer to New York, she smiled to herself. Finally, she and Malcolm would be together again. She could hardly wait!

There was no way for Paris to tell the future. But she was not afraid. Not anymore. The rough road she'd been on had led her to a stronger sense of herself. And though she was leaving the Lincoln home, she had their love to hold on to, as well as the lessons she'd learned while under their roof.

Paris had learned to keep God in her pocket, and as long as she kept him close, she knew she'd be all right.